D0563192

Lady Katherine only has one week to catch the Pink-Ribbon Killer. Not only to stop the killing, but also to prove her skills at detection to her father and win her dowry and independence.

There's only one catch—she has to take one last match-making job to do it. Never mind that the match is impossible—all the better because if she fails, then no one will seek her services again. The job provides the perfect cover, especially when her peculiar investigatory techniques are mistaken for unconventional match-making attempts.

Things would go a lot smoother if she weren't knee-deep in suspects and thwarted at every turn by a rival matchmaker. But when the killer strikes again, Katherine's investigation leads down a dangerous path. Too late, she discovers that she has a lot more to lose than her dowry.

AN INVITATION TO MURDER

LADY KATHERINE REGENCY MYSTERIES
(BOOK 1)

LEIGHANN DOBBS
HARMONY WILLIAMS

LEIGHANN DOBBS PUBLISHING

This is a work of fiction.

None of it is real. All names, places, and events are products of the author's imagination. Any resemblance to real names, places, or events are purely coincidental, and should not be construed as being real.

AN INVITATION TO MURDER

Copyright © 2017

Leighann Dobbs Publishing

http://www.leighanndobbs.com

All Rights Reserved.

No part of this work may be used or reproduced in any manner, except as allowable under "fair use," without the express written permission of the author.

 Created with Vellum

PREFACE

1816 England was a time of unrest. The end of the
Napoleonic Wars meant that London and other cities
were flooded with former soldiers now without jobs.
An increase of beggars, homeless, and other desperate
souls meant an increase in crime.

Fortunately, London had Sir John's Men to keep
the peace. Formed in 1754, Fielding's men—later
called Sir John's Men when he was knighted—were
more commonly, and derisively, referred to as the Bow
Street Runners. The precursors for the modern detective, there was a stigma against the investigative
sciences or "thief-takers" from the century before,
when corruption was rampant, and evidence fabri-
cated or bribes accepted to keep criminals out of
prison.

Therefore, although Sir John's Men did impeccable work, they were not well-respected nor was their profession thought of as respectable. It is for that reason that the Royal Society of Investigative Techniques, a fictional creation for the purposes of this story, is an underground club and Katherine must maintain a cover while she conducts an investigation.

Lady Katherine Irvine, the daughter of an earl, is in a different social class from the Bow Street Runners. For that reason, if it were widely known that she works undercover as a detective, she and her family would be disparaged by the ton.

The ton, also referred to as le bon ton, High Society, or Polite Society, are the old money of England, the rich and powerful with lineages dating back to the Dark Ages and the titles and lands that go along with such a prestigious bloodline.

The reputations of the young ladies in this social class hinge upon a misogynistic insistence upon "ladylike" or "acceptable" feminine behavior that Katherine defies at every turn because we, as the authors, think such constriction is a load of bollocks. One of the ways Katherine counteracts this expectation is by swearing using Regency terms such as "tarnation" and "sard," both unacceptable for the use of polite females. In her acceptance of friendship regardless social class,

Katherine is ahead of her time much the same way Lyle Murphy, the Bow Street Runner and inventor, is ahead of his time with some of his inventions.

Regardless of these intentional anachronisms, we hope that you enjoy the story!

CHAPTER ONE

Thursday, August 22, 1816.
Irvine House, London, England.

LADY KATHERINE IRVINE, daughter of the Earl of Dorchester who was one of the most brilliant detective minds of Britain, stared the villain in the eye and pointed at the toe of her embroidered slipper. "Drop it, thief, or you won't like the consequences."

Her pet pug, Emma, spat out the slim leather-bound notebook and wagged her curly tail. Her dark eyes glimmered with mischief.

"Good girl. Come here and I'll give you a rub."

As Katherine knelt to retrieve her notes on the hair-raising murder case that had eluded even her father, Emma hunched down with her tail in the air. The dog snatched the notebook and made off with it.

"That isn't a toy!" Katherine hiked her dove-gray skirts to her knees and still managed to trip over an errant obstacle. Her bedchamber was riddled with them. Her notes on the recent deluge of crime in and around London decorated every available surface, including the floor. It made for slippery footing.

She winced at the crumple of paper as she landed on one knee, worried that she had destroyed her theories on the Pink-Ribbon Murders.

Two young debutantes murdered at two separate house parties had the *ton* so up in arms that they'd cancelled their remaining events. Katherine thought it was a sensible decision, for with the crime scenes disturbed and the guests too deep in their cups or entrenched in frivolity to recall much at all, even Papa hadn't been able to solve the murders.

But Katherine would. She and her father had a wager. If she could solve a murder case on her own before her twenty-fifth birthday, which was in fewer than ten days, he would award her with her dowry to use however she pleased.

It would please her greatly to depart from her father's and stepmother's incessant cooing as they snuck about in a last attempt to give the earldom an heir. It would be all the better if she could manage such independence without having to rely on anyone but herself.

However, Emma could shred Katherine's hopes just as easily as the notebook she held between her teeth. Katherine had poured the bulk of her theories on the Pink-Ribbon Murders into that book.

"Emma." Her voice held a note of warning, not that the little pug took heed in any way. The dog dove beneath the coverlet, which hung askew off the bed. It seemed the dog thought she was out of sight and out of mind, for Emma didn't seem to notice that her backside wasn't quite as warm as her front. Her tail wagged vigorously in the open air above her golden rump.

Holding her breath, Katherine crept near her. *Please don't chew on those notes,* she prayed. *I'll never give you another bone if you do.*

Two steps remained between her and the ornery dog. Then one.

As she bent to seize Emma's back end, the dog scurried farther beneath the bed. Katherine lowered herself, flattened on her stomach, and wriggled in after Emma, her arms outstretched. Her hips became wedged between the ground and the low bedframe, immobilizing her.

"Oh, tarnation!" She and her oldest sister had both

inherited her late mother's figure, wider in the hips than around the chest. She didn't fit beneath the bed. "That deuced dog!"

With a short, plaintive whine, Emma halted her retreat just out of reach and dropped the notebook. *Blessed be!* If Katherine could only reach a little farther...

The door latch jiggled. Muffled footsteps stopped abruptly. From behind her, a familiar voice exclaimed, "Lady Katherine! What have you done to this room?"

Eureka, she had something! Katherine gripped the slippery item between her fingers and drew back so quickly that she walloped her head on the hard wooden bedframe. Wincing, she sat back on her heels and held up her prize, triumphant.

What she held was not a notebook, but the puce silk ribbon her lady's maid, Harriet, had tied around Emma's neck. "Sard it all," Katherine swore.

Harriet's expression turned every bit as dark as her hair. "You're learning too much foul language from your Bow Street Runner friend."

Katherine raised an eyebrow. Her foray beneath the bed had caused several locks of brown hair to fall out of her coif and into her eyes. She brushed them aside with her free hand. "I believe he prefers to be called one of Sir John's men."

"I believe he prefers to be called Lyle," Harriet countered. She stepped forward, her hands on her round hips. "Now, what are you doing beneath the bed, my lady?"

With a disgusted sigh, Katherine rose and dusted off her dress. "Emma's stolen something again."

"It must be something important."

"My notebook, the one I've been using to record my ideas on the Pink-Ribbon Murders."

Harriet tossed her thick braid over one shoulder. "I know the one. Why don't I find it for you while you attend to your guest?"

Katherine didn't care for the falsely sweet smile her longtime maid wore, nor for the twinkle in her ebony eyes.

"Is Lyle here?" she asked as she raked her gaze over Harriet's attire. She wore a faded sunshine-yellow dress, one of Katherine's cast-offs. Nothing about her appearance indicated that she had formed a sudden tendre for Katherine's dearest friend, which was a pity. Lyle could use a guiding hand.

"Are you expecting him?" Harriet asked, her voice as sweet as her smile. "I'll fix your hair if you'd care to go down."

"No need." Katherine used the ribbon in her hand to tie back the errant strands of hair. "Help me catch that thieving dog. Lyle and I have an investigative society meeting to attend tonight, and I cannot be late." Not only did she owe a colleague her notes on a case he had trouble pursuing, but she wanted to learn as much as she could about the Pink-Ribbon Murders. The next society meeting wouldn't be for a month.

Harriet retrieved a foot-long brass shoehorn from near the wardrobe and approached the bed, bending as if she meant to sweep it underneath like a broom. Katherine took up a post on the opposite side.

In a casual tone, the maid added, "I fear you'll be late even if we manage to wrangle Emma into behaving."

Katherine chewed on her lower lip as she bent to peer beneath the lip of the bed once more. All she saw were the lamplight reflections of two beady eyes squarely under the center of the large mattress and out of reach. With disgust, she let the coverlet drop into place.

She had more important matters to which to attend, such as the bevy of notes scattered across the room. *Oh dear.* Perhaps she would be late, after all. Abandoning her post, she hurried to collect the pages. She skimmed each, searching for the ones pertaining to tonight's meeting.

Her efforts to solve the Pink-Ribbon Murders

would be much more fruitful if the string of house parties was to continue—and if she could have somehow secured an invitation without having to pretend to join the husband hunt. How tedious.

"Perhaps we can entice Emma out with a treat," Katherine said absentmindedly. The drawer to her writing desk creaked as she opened it to stuff the pages out of sight. Lodged in one corner was the reticule packed full of dried dog treats. As she plucked it out, Katherine put on a wheedling tone. "Would you like that, Emma, darling, to be rewarded for your misbehavior?"

Harriet snorted as she straightened. She tossed the shoehorn onto the mattress with a wry shake of the head. "She's a dog, my lady. She doesn't understand English."

"Nonsense." Katherine dipped her fingers between the strings of the reticule to break off a small morsel of the dried meat in the pouch. "She understands plenty of English words. Ball, walk, supper, bed."

Dusting off her hands, Harriet said, "Well, in that case, perhaps she'll understand when I tell her that if she doesn't come out of there, I'll see she's made into cat food!"

Katherine laughed as she returned the treat bag to

the drawer, not expecting an answer from the threatened canine. To her surprise, Emma yipped as she scurried out from beneath the bed. She barreled toward Katherine, tripping over her short legs along the way. As she scrambled to get all her feet under her before she sat, she tipped her eager face up and let her pink tongue loll out the side of her mouth. The notebook was nowhere to be seen.

"Please tell me you haven't eaten it," Katherine muttered as she knelt to feed her pet the morsel. Emma lapped it up and sniffed her hands for more.

Meanwhile, Harriet crouched to peek under the bed. "It's under here. Why don't you entertain Mrs. Pickering while I fetch it for you and straighten up?"

"Mrs. Pickering?" Katherine searched out the sensitive spot behind Emma's ear. The dog thumped her foot on the floor in glee. Katherine groped for another fallen sheaf of notes with her free hand.

Her voice muffled, the maid answered from her position halfway under the bed, "Indeed. She called asking after your expertise."

"Mine?" Katherine straightened, fighting a smile as she clutched the papers to her chest. "Not Papa's?" She wondered how Mrs. Pickering could have learned about her. The daughters of earls did not openly solve crimes, not even when said earl was known for his eccentricities.

Harriet resurfaced with the notebook in hand. She stood too far away for Katherine to judge whether or not the notes within would still be legible, but Katherine was not worried. Emma had a gentle touch and tended to use her lips instead of her teeth when absconding with precious objects.

Smirking, Harriet answered, "I doubt your father would prove a very good matchmaker."

Katherine froze and turned to her maid with a scowl. "Matchmaking?" The word tasted foul. "No. Never again. Send her away."

As Katherine's attention waned, Emma returned to her mischief by vigorously smelling the nearest page of notes. Oh, no she wouldn't! Katherine grasped her around her middle and lifted her, thrusting her out in front of her as she crossed the room.

Tapping the leather-bound book idly against her palm, Harriet looked smug. "I tried telling her you were not at home, but she insisted upon waiting for your return. She's heard so much about your success with your sisters."

Katherine narrowed her eyes. "Is this punishment for messing up my room?"

Harriet laughed. "It's the truth. Go downstairs and see for yourself."

The sky would freeze over before Katherine did that. She thrust Emma into her maid's arms. "Trade me that book for this ornery dog."

"Of course, my lady. We'll have *heaps* of fun together."

The moment Harriet clasped the pug's middle, Emma pumped her legs as if hoping to outrun her in midair.

Katherine examined the book and found it no worse for wear. *Thank Zeus.* Katherine carefully inserted the notebook into her bulging reticule.

Balancing the feisty dog on her hip, Harriet added, "I sent a pot of tea in to warm Mrs. Pickering, but that's bound to get cold if you tarry too much longer."

Katherine glared. "I shan't be meeting with her, nor taking a confounded matchmaking job."

"Not even if she pays you? I'd do it."

Katherine wasn't quite that desperate to leave her father's house. She could wait nine days for her dowry, when she'd have funds aplenty to let a cozy townhouse of her own.

"If you're so eager, then why don't you take the job?" Turning, Katherine gathered up the last of the pages and thumbed through them to find the particular notes she needed.

"I would, but I seem to have my hands full."

When Katherine offered her friend an arch stare, Harriet lifted the pug as if offering proof.

"I'll be late to my meeting with Lyle if I don't depart immediately."

Harriet shrugged. "Very well. If you mean to avoid her, you'll have to go out the window. She's in the blue parlor, next to the door."

Harriet must have seated her in such a central location on purpose. Katherine glared.

Her smile widening, Harriet added, "Don't fret. I left Lyle in with her for entertainment."

Katherine's heart skipped a beat. "Please tell me you're jesting."

"Not at all. Best not keep them waiting."

Egads, what could Lyle have found to talk about— the rate of decay of a drowned corpse? The smell and consistency of rat droppings if poison had been ingested? The only thing her dear friend did worse than making small talk was flirting.

Although Mrs. Pickering wasn't the most powerful of her peers, she had enough clout to wrangle a Season for her daughter, which made her far more powerful than the Bow Street Runners, up at whom she no doubt turned her nose.

"Ensure Emma doesn't steal my notes," Katherine ordered, breathless. Before Lyle caused an incident that might reflect poorly on her and cause Papa to retract his wager for her dowry, she bolted down two flights of stairs and into the blue parlor.

The moment she entered the room, she found Lyle's long-limbed form squeezed into a spindly chintz-upholstered chair better suited to a lady's frame. He held a delicate teacup between two fingers as if it would attack him. His carrot-colored hair stuck out in all directions, and splotches of pink obscured the freckles on his cheeks.

Katherine pinned a smile in place, though inwardly she quavered. "How nice to see you, Mrs. Pickering. Please forgive the delay."

"No need," Lyle said, his voice weak as he stood from the chair. He still handled the teacup as if it would shatter with any greater force. "We entertained ourselves with a scintillating conversation about"—he glanced at Mrs. Pickering and swallowed visibly, his Adam's apple bobbing—"ladies' undergarments."

Good grief! How had he managed that?

"Harriet's begged me to convince you to let her straighten your cravat. She's up on the third floor."

Bald relief crossed his face. He set the teacup on the table, bending nearly in half to do so. Not many men stretched as tall as Lyle, nor managed to look so gangly in the process. With his lack of coordination and absentminded air, he half reminded her of a marionette, not that she would ever insult him to his face.

As he tripped over his tongue excusing himself, Katherine held out the sheaf of papers she'd collected. "Would you mind looking after these for me? I shan't be long."

"Of course." He bolted from the room, pulling at the cravat he wore only for society meetings.

Katherine lowered herself into his seat. The moment her rump kissed the chair, Mrs. Pickering's manner turned from ennui to accusation.

"If you thought sending him in as entertainment would dissuade me from staying, you are wrong."

What else did he talk about before settling on undergarments? Knowing Lyle, the topics were inexhaustible. He was one of the most brilliant minds she knew. Unfortunately, a flair for inventions and investigations did not lend itself to easy manners.

Katherine didn't have time for an argument. She clasped her hands in her lap. "I'm afraid I'm not taking on matchmaking clients at this time. Thank you for your inquiry, but I must insist that you find someone else."

A look of panic crossed Mrs. Pickering's face. As Katherine started to rise, the older woman—nearing fifty, by Katherine's estimate—laid her hand over Katherine's on her lap, thereby pinning her in place.

"Please, hear out my offer. I beg of you."

Katherine tried to harden her heart against the note of desperation in the woman's demeanor. She wasn't the only matchmaking mama to despair of making an advantageous marriage for her daughter. Although Katherine tried to disentangle herself, the woman's grip was like iron.

"Madam, please—"

"We'll pay. Whatever fee you name."

The woman's fingernails dug into Katherine's skin. With a wince, she glanced down just as Mrs. Pickering retracted her hand. Her fingernails were not buffed. The edges were a bit tattered, as if she did manual labor.

Impossible... or was it? Her fingernails weren't the only sign of wear. Her threadbare dress hung loose, as if she'd lost weight. It was darned in places along the sleeve, a testament to how often she wore it. Her slippers were scuffed, some of the embroidery coming loose or fraying. She wore no jewelry save for the modest wedding ring she twisted on her left hand—no earrings, no necklace. And judging by the slackness in the reticule hanging from her wrist, she didn't carry much about her person.

These signs, coupled with the pronounced worry lines around her eyes and nose, indicated that Mrs. Pickering was a step away from poverty. Her polite façade covered more desperation than that for her daughter.

Katherine's resolve to send her away floundered.

After pressing her lips together, her nostrils flaring, Mrs. Pickering said, "You found such wonderful matches for your sisters. Love matches, even."

Katherine's motives had been selfish. If her stepmother, Susanna, had a wedding to plan, she wouldn't have time to turn her matrimonial eye to Katherine. Also, she would have more time alone with her father to learn the nuances of their chosen profession.

"Please, you're my last hope," Mrs. Pickering begged. "This is Annie's only Season. If she isn't wed soon..."

Katherine didn't want to hear about Mrs. Pickering's financial difficulties. If she hadn't thrown her daughter a Season, her funds likely would have lasted years. With the fashions and entertainments, a London Season cost a small fortune. Once she was financially independent, such frivolity would be the first thing she cut from her budget. And now the Season had been cut short.

"The Season is over, madam. Everyone and their dogs have retreated to their country estates. I don't know what you'd have me do."

Hope broke through Mrs. Pickering's expression like the sun through clouds. "The Earl of Northbrook is throwing a house party as planned. Rumor has it his mother is bent upon marrying him off so he can beget the estate an heir this year. Annie could be that wife, if only you'll agree to help."

When she reached forward to clasp Katherine's hands again, Katherine moved them out of reach. "I wish you the best of luck, but the answer remains—"

Wait. A house party? She frowned. Papa had obtained a thorough guest list from the last two house parties, and both lists had contained the names of fatalities.

"Was Lord Northbrook one of those who attended the Duke of Somerset's house party?" That had been the first murder.

Mrs. Pickering nodded. "He was. Such a shame about that poor girl. And he was at the second calamity as well. I feared that would be the end of our plan to extend the Season into the country." She pressed her lips together, her eyes clouding over. "If not for our situation, I'd never let Annie attend another house party this summer. But..."

Katherine's trepidation faded in the swell of jubilance that overcame her. Papa had claimed that he would be unable to solve the Pink-Ribbon Murders because the Season had been cut short. No more parties meant no more opportunities to observe suspects and, of course, no more opportunities for the killer to strike again.

Although she didn't wish for more deaths, surely gathering together the guests once more would give her an opportunity to solve the murders herself! She bit the inside of her cheek to keep from grinning, an uncouth reaction given the gravity of the circumstances.

"There's one problem," she said, hoping that Mrs. Pickering would have a solution. "After Lord Somerset's party, I tried to get an invitation to the next, but I was declined, seeing as the tour was already underway. How do you propose I gain entry to Lord Northbrook's party?"

Mrs. Pickering's face lit up. The worry etched into her wrinkles faded away as optimism spilled from her pores. "If that is your only concern, give it no thought at all. I'll pretend to be sick, and you can take my place as Annie's chaperone."

Perhaps there was some merit to this matchmaking job after all. It was a small price to pay if it would help her earn her dowry.

Katherine held out her hand. "Very well, Mrs. Pickering. I accept."

CHAPTER TWO

O f all the streets in London, Katherine wondered why Pall Mall Street had to be one of the first to be fixed with gas-lit street lamps.

She swore under her breath, trying to skirt the brighter-than-average light so she could cling to Lyle's shadow. Considering that he stood no more than a hand taller than her and was much thinner, his form didn't help to camouflage hers.

Not for the first time, she wished for her sisters' slight heights. Even in a gray dress that blended with the twilight shadows, Katherine was far too recognizable. An earl's daughter shouldn't be seen alone with a man late at night. Although Katherine didn't care a whit for the *ton*'s gossip about her, she didn't want her notoriety to reflect poorly on her sisters.

Lyle glanced over at her quirky movements as she tried to keep to his shadow and laughed. "You're far more conspicuous while trying not to be noticed than you would be if you'd only walk next to me like usual."

"Why in tarnation would the founders think it's a splendid idea to host secret-society meetings on such a busy street?"

"Gas lights didn't exist when the society was founded. Besides, if you'd been a bit quicker, we might have been able to reach the meeting before the lamps were lit for the night."

He was right. If Emma and Mrs. Pickering hadn't delayed her, they might have arrived half an hour earlier.

Lyle lengthened his stride to step over a puddle. When he offered his hand, she handed him the sheaf of papers, lifted her skirt above her ankles, and hopped over the obstacle by her own merit. Her friend returned the pages without comment.

As they resumed their quick gait, he asked, "Why did Mrs. Pickering seek you out?"

"How do you know she didn't come knocking on my door to speak of lady's undergarments?"

Lyle turned as red as a plum and tried to hide his face beneath the fringe of his hair. "I merely had a question to further my research. Perhaps it was a bit inappropriate."

Katherine took pity on him and added, "She has a matchmaking job for me."

"Ah. So you had to turn her away."

"Quite the contrary. I accepted."

Lyle looked incredulous. "Accepted? But you're no matchmaker."

Katherine reared up. "I did admirably with my sisters. But I don't mean to facilitate the match if I can help it. If I'm known for anything, I do not want it to be for matchmaking."

"Then why pretend?"

She hugged the papers to her chest. "The Pink-Ribbon Murders, of course."

Lyle nodded. "Ah. I see."

"I've only nine days to solve a case for Papa, and accepting the matchmaking proposal is my only way in."

Lyle motioned for her to precede him up the stairs, and she hurried to the door. A footman posted inside opened it for her and offered to take her shawl. She declined.

Once she and Lyle were out of earshot and strolling the length of the narrow, dimly lit corridor that led toward the back stairs, he continued the conversation. "Why is that your only way to investigate?"

"I'm having trouble obtaining invites to these infernal parties. The matchmaking excuse may be the only chance to get most of the people that were at both parties in the same place."

Lyle mulled that over. "Yes, with precious little evidence, it would be beneficial to observe the suspects. Maybe the killer will give himself away somehow."

Precious little evidence? Everything Katherine knew about the murders had come from her father, but maybe Lyle knew something more. "What do you know of the Pink-Ribbon Murders?"

To her disappointment, he answered, "I don't know much, I'm afraid. A pair of Sir John's men were invited to Somerset's estate after the guests had departed. I wasn't one of them. From what I hear, there was little to glean by then. No suspects, no witnesses, and the body had been moved and washed. All I know is that the crime occurred in the garden, where the victim was strangled using a pink ribbon off her own dress."

"The killer used her own ribbon, you say?" Katherine frowned. "Miss Rosehill, the second victim, was also strangled with a pink ribbon, but she was wearing yellow. It wasn't hers."

"How do you know?"

"Papa drove up to the second estate. Our family has ties to Miss Rosehill, though I've only met her once." Katherine's heart squeezed at the image of the cheerful young blonde. "Papa investigated out of courtesy, but he wasn't able to find anything more. Like you said, the body had been moved, and the crime scene was contaminated from people coming and going. He conducted a cursory interview, but by the time he arrived, the guests were already departing. He didn't learn enough to narrow the list of suspects."

"So the killer brought the ribbon. That may show premeditation." Lyle pursed his lips and turned to her. "He may kill again. Promise me you'll be careful."

"I promise."

"I'll ask my friend who went up to Somerset's estate for more details. If you need me, send for me."

Katherine raised an eyebrow. "I have to solve this murder on my own in order to meet my father's criteria, remember?"

He dropped his hand. "Perhaps, but I doubt he means for you to get hurt in the process. Would you like to use any of my inventions?"

Lyle had created so many inventions to aid in forensic investigations that she couldn't think of which might benefit her most. Many of them required more trunk space than she would have. "Thank you, yes. But anything I bring will have to fit in my trunk, and please, no prototypes. I don't want to risk breaking your only device."

He smiled. "I'm not worried. I can always make another."

Perhaps, but his prototypes don't always perform as planned. She didn't want to destroy evidence or roast her fingers.

"Are you available tomorrow to show me what you've made and how it works?" Katherine would insist upon a demonstration, just in case.

"If you call before noon. I'm nearly finished with the formula for a dye that will help adhere to the residue left when someone touches fabric. You know, I've been examining my findings, and if you look closely enough, there are subtle intricacies in the imprint left by a finger."

Katherine cut him off, as they were running late enough that they might miss tonight's meeting entirely. "Perhaps you can show me tomorrow?"

"Oh, yes, of course. Shall we?" He gestured to the staircase.

They ascended to the second floor, where most of the members gathered. The upstairs rooms had sparse furniture, cleared to ensure there would be enough space for everyone. Because members from all walks of life were encouraged to attend, the number often grew unruly. Judging by the resounding chatter and the way the members, mostly male, were clumped into groups and carrying on their own conversations, she and Lyle had missed the official bulletin of today's meeting.

"I need to find Colonel Grant and pass along these notes."

He nodded and remained at her elbow while she circulated throughout the room. Although she stopped to greet the members she and her father knew—most of the people in the room—Lyle remained her stiff, mute shadow. By the time she delivered the pages and discussed her thoughts with the colonel, Lyle didn't appear to be paying any attention to the others in room at all.

At least, to no one in the room, save for one. His attention was rapt on one corner of the room, where Lady Philomena Graylocke, the Duchess of Tenwick, sat with an ebony-haired toddler on her lap as she spoke with unconcealed enthusiasm about her inventions of late. She'd gathered more than a few admirers to take part in the discussion. Due to the limited seats near her, most stood around her on either side.

Katherine elbowed Lyle in the ribs before he started drooling.

He sighed. "She's beautiful."

"Miss Graylocke? I think she's a little young for you."

Lyle glared at Katherine. "Not the child. Her mother."

Katherine fought a smirk. Phil was the sort of woman to light up a room, as much with her intelligence and wit as her beauty. A decade older than Katherine, the duchess hadn't yet started to show signs of worry or age despite her rambunctious children. Her brown hair was untouched with gray, and only the hint of laugh lines around the impish curve of her mouth belied that she was older than Katherine.

Unfortunately for Lyle, Phil's happily married state put her firmly beyond his reach. That didn't keep him from swooning over her every time they crossed paths.

"Why don't you go talk to her?"

"Because the duke will rip me limb from limb?"

Katherine laughed. "I didn't say flirt with her." *My, that would be a sight!* Katherine had seen pigeons flirt with more success. "Speak to her. Ask after her inventions."

The color fled his cheeks as he shook his head. "I couldn't. She's a duchess, and what am I? A lowly Bow Street Runner."

Katherine tapped him on the arm. "Don't say that. You're one of Sir John's men, and that's a position to be proud of. You keep the streets of London safe."

"Not safe enough, given all the crime that has cropped up since the end of the war."

"You do your part. More than that, in fact. If not for your inventions, how many crimes would go unsolved?"

His cheeks turned a bit pink, though it was difficult to tell in the light of the hearth fire whether that was due to flattery or embarrassment. "My inventions are useful, I suppose," he mumbled.

"More than useful, they're brilliant. You and Phil have that in common." Katherine latched onto his arm as if he were a gentleman and she were a conventional lady. "Come, tell Phil about that new dye you've been concocting."

The sound Lyle made was more reminiscent of her dog than a human, but he didn't fight her as she led the way to the corner of the room. Katherine dropped his arm as they neared, the better to approach the duchess as equals.

"Phil, so nice to see you tonight," Katherine said, her voice warm. Now that she was near, she realized that Phil might be precisely the person she should question about investigative methods before she departed for Lord Northbrook's house party.

Phil had once confessed to her that she had worked to catch a French spy and turn the tide of the war. A terribly thrilling tale! Katherine could use greater insight on the matter of the Pink-Ribbon Murders.

The duchess smiled. "And you, Katherine. Did your father come with you?"

"No, I'm here with my friend Lyle Murphy tonight. Mr. Murphy, this is Lady Philomena Gray-locke, as I'm sure you know."

Keeping one hand around her small daughter's middle to keep the child balanced, Phil leaned forward and offered Lyle her hand. "Lovely to meet you, Mr. Murphy. And please, my friends call me Phil."

Flushing with as much color as his hair, Lyle bent to kiss Phil's knuckles. He must have thought better of it halfway through, because he wound up kissing the air and giving her hand a little shake at the same time. Katherine had never seen a more awkward greeting. He turned a deep shade of plum as he straightened.

Hoping to give him time to recover, Katherine added, "Mr. Murphy is an investigator with Sir John's men. His inventions have aided their efforts greatly.

Mr. Murphy, why don't you tell her about your newest invention, the one you mentioned to me earlier?"

Katherine worried that if Lyle didn't take a breath soon, he was going to turn blue. He stumbled over his tongue, mumbling something about clothing and touching. After his jumbled attempt at conversation, he abruptly bowed and excused himself, turning on his heel before Katherine could grab his elbow and convince him to stay.

Phil frowned as she watched him depart. "Oh dear. I didn't offend him, did I?"

Staring at the path he'd taken, Katherine warred with the desire to follow him and make certain he was all right. However, she needed Phil's advice, and tonight might be the only time she would be able to attain it. Lyle was a grown man and could take care of himself.

Perching on the edge of an ottoman across from Phil, she answered, "He isn't accustomed to interacting with the *ton*. I hope you'll forgive his abruptness."

"Of course. I didn't mean to intimidate him."

Katherine smiled. Phil was one of the most unaffected people she knew, as was the rest of the Graylocke family. Though she was a duchess, she never put on airs, and always spoke to others as equals.

"It isn't your fault, I'm certain."

Perched on her mother's lap, Miss Graylocke made a burbling noise as she fit two pieces of an intricate wooden puzzle together.

Katherine smiled at the little girl, who appeared too caught up in her task to notice her audience. "What do you have there?"

"It's a puzzle I created," Phil answered. "She loves them. When this one is fitted together properly, it will become a ball. You watch, she'll have it figured out by the end of the evening."

"What an intelligent young woman."

Phil glowed at the praise. "She takes after her father."

No doubt she had no small part of her mother in her as well, though Phil was too modest to admit it.

"How have you been?" the duchess asked.

"I'm well. I took your advice and asked Papa for a chance to earn my dowry. I have nine days to solve a mystery, and he'll award it to me."

Phil beamed. "That's fantastic. I'm certain you'll finish with time to spare."

"Perhaps, but I could use your advice."

Miss Graylocke dropped one of her puzzle pieces. Katherine fished it off the ground, dusted it off, and returned it to the child. She received a soft word of thanks in exchange.

Smiling fondly at her daughter, Phil asked, "Advice concerning what?"

"Investigative techniques. I mean to do my own search for a criminal who has eluded even my father. I know you've conducted such a search before. How do you recommend I find him?"

Phil leaned back, a pensive expression on her face. Upon seeing that her attention was fixed elsewhere, members of her admiring audience started conversations among themselves or wandered away.

Katherine paid them no mind; Phil's opinion mattered most to her. Phil had conducted independent investigations in the past, and as a woman, she had faced the same societal limitations on her movements as Katherine.

After a moment, the duchess answered, "The best proof is through confession. Sometimes, the evidence is so elusive that you have nothing more than your own suspicions on which to rely. You've been doing this for a long time, perhaps even longer than me."

"I'm flattered, but I've always had my father around to lead the investigation."

Phil tucked one of her daughter's curls behind the child's ear. "Perhaps you have, but you've been a fixture at your father's side ever since I've known you. That experience means you know enough to formulate your own theories. Listen to your instincts. I'm certain they won't lead you astray."

Katherine's chest warmed knowing that an accomplished woman of Phil's caliber had faith in her. "So I'll need to goad the criminal into confessing."

"Not necessarily," Phil cautioned, "but it is often the best way to be sure. While I was hunting that spy years ago, Morgan and I actually thought her to be the French spymaster at first, before we infiltrated her home and recovered evidence that suggested she was answering to someone else. Even though we didn't find the proof we thought we were looking for, we found a clue that pointed us in the right direction. It was Morgan's sister who eventually found and caught the true spymaster."

That wouldn't do at all. In order to attain her independence, Katherine needed to capture the Pink-Ribbon Killer herself. If she were to do that and could get a confession, that would be best, as it would eliminate any shadow of doubt. But in order to get that confession, maybe she would need some sort of evidence, like what Phil had obtained with the spy, in order to coerce the confession.

"Does that help?" Phil asked.

"It does. At the very least, it gives me a goal as I

start my investigation. Thank you. Your advice, as always, is invaluable."

Katherine stood and smiled as Miss Graylocke fitted the last piece of her puzzle together, which formed a ball the size of her two fists. With luck, Katherine would soon be every bit as triumphant.

CHAPTER THREE

Two days later.
The Earl of Northbrook's Estate.

WHEN KATHERINE ACCEPTED this matchmaking job, even just as a cover to conduct her investigation, she hadn't realized how hopeless her task would be.

Miss Annie Pickering lovingly laid out a collection of dead insects pinned to slices of wood. *Her valise must be bottomless for her to be able to fit so many grotesque specimens inside.* As the plump young woman, only a couple years younger than Katherine, bent over the valise to choose yet another preserved butterfly, Katherine cleared her throat. "Miss Pickering."

With a broad smile displaying a charming gap in her front teeth and a pair of dimples, the young woman straightened. She clutched the specimen proudly. "Call me Annie, please. I feel as though we're already friends."

Katherine fought the urge to pinch the bridge of her nose. As her charge laid the insect on the coverlet of her bed alongside a dozen others, Katherine said, "I was asked here as your chaperone to help you draw the earl's eye."

The color drained from Annie's flushed cheeks, leaving the smattering of freckles across her nose and cheeks more noticeable. She sat heavily on the mattress. Her sea-green skirt narrowly missed the nearest butterfly.

The color of her dress, subtly darned in places though showing less wear than her mother's, made her eyes seem an even more brilliant shade of green. That was, when one could see them behind the unruly mop of brown hair. Annie brushed aside the errant strands and beseeched Katherine with her gaze. "I know Mama hired you to help the match. Do you..." Her chin wobbled. "Do you think there's any hope at all?" She glanced down, twisting her skirt in her hands.

Katherine's heart echoed the gesture, twisting at the sight of Annie's despair. *Tarnation!* She wasn't supposed to care about the outcome of this match-making job. When faced with Annie's innocent hopes, Katherine couldn't help but want her to succeed.

How am I supposed to marry a penniless insect-lover to an earl? Perhaps, once she'd caught the Pink-Ribbon Killer, she would find a way.

After gingerly clearing a spot to sit, she perched on the mattress next to Annie and took one of the young woman's hands in hers, squeezing. "Of course there is hope. I've spent five minutes with you, and I can already tell you have a good heart."

Despite the compliment, Annie's face fell. She fingered the edge of an orange-winged butterfly with black markings along its top edge and gruesome blue spots that resembled eyes in the bottom swell. "It's beautiful, isn't it?"

From afar. Katherine forced a smile. "Quite lovely." She would count her blessings if she didn't have nightmares from this.

With a fond smile, Annie continued to stroke the wing as she explained, "It doesn't start out that way. In fact, as a caterpillar, it's rather fat and ugly. It becomes something beautiful along the way." Eyes shining, she met Katherine's gaze.

"You don't need to become someone else in order

to catch Lord Northbrook's eye. All we need to do is ensure that he sees the kindhearted woman you are."

Annie managed a shaky smile. "Do you think?"

"I know. You forget, I've done this before." *With an earl's daughters who had substantial dowries.* In the end, both her sisters' husbands had grown to cherish their wives, but Katherine had to admit that the draw of their status, family connections, and fortunes made it much easier to draw the eyes of their husbands-to-be. And neither of them had been set on one man in particular.

Don't despair. After all, her true purpose in attending this party was to catch a murderer. Certainly, that took precedence. This matter of match-making... She couldn't afford to think about it until after she had apprehended the person responsible for killing two women.

Putting distance between her and the eerie insects on the bed, Katherine stood. "Did you need to bring quite so many of... those?"

Annie snatched up one of her specimens and held it defensively to her chest. "I need them."

Katherine couldn't think of any possible use for a collection of dead vermin. She held her arms akimbo. "Why?"

"Because I do. What if someone asks to see my collection?"

"No one will ask."

Her eyelashes fluttering, Annie looked down at the pest in her hand. The bulk of her hair fell into her eyes again. "Someone might ask," she said in a small voice.

Her collection would scandalize most of the guests and certainly was not ladylike or appealing to prospective husbands, so Katherine hoped that the topic would not arise. "No one will think that you've carried your entire collection to Lord Northbrook's house."

Annie brushed the hair out of her eyes. "This isn't my entire collection. I also have dozens of live specimens."

Her mother must be a saint! Katherine drew herself up. "Please keep your collection confined to your room."

With a vigorous nod, the young woman agreed. "Yes, of course. I'll keep them safe here."

It would be wrong of Katherine to hide them for the duration of the house party, and that would require touching them, which she preferred to avoid even if they were dead. Best to let Annie keep them confined to her room.

"Where is my peacock butterfly?"

Katherine's heart skipped a beat. *Please tell me it*

did not reanimate and fly away. Fearfully, she scanned the room, only to catch a glimpse of a wagging golden tail a moment before Emma disappeared into the adjoining chamber.

"Emma!" *If that blasted dog has developed a taste for insects and starts hoarding them in her room like bones...* Katherine shuddered and took off, skidding into the other chamber, the one assigned to her as Annie's chaperone, to search for her pet pug.

Smirking, Harriet caught the thief around the middle seconds before the dog dove beneath the neatly made bed. She balanced her on one hip as she bravely detached the insect from Emma's teeth. Tongue lolling, Emma wagged her tail, proud of herself.

Harriet held the butterfly out to Annie, who had followed on Katherine's heels. The young woman exclaimed and vigorously checked the dead insect for injury. Thankfully, Emma's light touch with her treasures meant that the insect had merely suffered a little dampness caused by Emma's tongue.

Katherine herded her toward her room once more. "Why don't you put that away? I imagine most of the guests will have arrived by now. They're likely down with the hostess at afternoon tea. We should join them."

Annie froze in place, blinking owlishly between

strands of hair. "The hostess. Do you mean Lord Northbrook's mother? I hear she's frighteningly exacting over the sort of woman her son marries."

To the contrary, Katherine had heard that the dowager was desperate to see her son married off and producing children. She couldn't very well be both.

Instead of correcting the young woman, Katherine hoped to use Annie's trepidation to spur her from the room faster. "In that case, you ought not to be tardy. If you're the last to arrive, it might reflect poorly on us."

With a squeak, Annie disappeared into her room. Katherine followed to find her frantically searching for her slippers. She hopped on one foot as she donned one, and on the other foot while pulling on the other.

Behind her, Harriet chuckled. "No need to panic. You'll both head below in a trice."

Annie lost her balance and fell on her rump. She winced. From the cradle of Harriet's arms, Emma barked and squirmed, begging to be let down. Katherine would have held her captive, but her maid capitulated. The pug scrambled across the room to lick Annie's face. Katherine grabbed the pug, rescuing the poor young woman. Balancing Emma on her hip, she used her free hand to fish a handkerchief out of her reticule.

"Thank you," Annie said. Her words were muffled as she wiped her face clean.

"Why don't I fix your hair?" Harriet asked.

Katherine patted her coif, which seemed to be in place. "Am I out of sorts?"

"Not you," Harriet said, laughing. "Miss Pickering."

"Oh. That's a splendid idea."

Armed with an ivory-backed brush, Harriet rounded the young woman, who was still seated on the floor and seemed confused at the new turn of events. Katherine bit back a smile.

With a note of warning in her voice, Harriet brandished the brush and said, "Hold still. We'll have you ready before you know it."

Self-consciously, Annie patted down her hair as Katherine escorted her out of their room on the second floor of the manor and toward the stairs. "I still think I'd look better if I ornamented my hair. I have a male Chalk Hill blue butterfly in my room that would—"

"No." Katherine held up her hand, stalling whatever horrid suggestion Annie might think to add. "I draw the line at putting insects in your hair."

"But... I'm not pretty without it."

Much prettier than if she put vermin in her locks. Katherine could only begin to imagine the *ton*'s reaction to *that*.

In her opinion, the simple coiffure that Harriet had wrought did wonders to improve Annie's appearance. It better displayed the freckles adorning her round cheeks, but it also revealed her eyes, which Katherine considered to be Annie's crowning feature. When she was excited, they sparkled.

At that moment, they appeared sad and flat.

"What if he doesn't notice me? He hasn't so far this Season."

Katherine patted the young woman's arm, hoping to reassure her. "Be polite, be gracious. I'm certain you'll make a favorable impression upon both hosts."

Annie's fears didn't seem to be allayed, but as a door opened farther along the corridor, Katherine cut the conversation short. She laid a guiding hand on Annie's elbow, hoping to hurry her down the stairs.

"Lady Katherine."

A woman's voice dripped with scorn. Grimacing, Katherine turned to face Mrs. Fairchild. She'd had the misfortune of crossing paths with the professional matchmaker while attempting to find husbands for her sisters. Apparently, her success in those instances had made her an enemy.

Despite the fact that she couldn't be more than ten years older than Katherine, if that, Mrs. Fairchild held herself as if she carried a lifetime's more experience. Her auburn hair was pulled back in a severe style and covered with a lace cap. Her cerulean dress covered her from wrist to neck to ankle. Despite the unfashionable color, the matchmaker wore the dress as if it were the crown jewels. She cultivated a haughty air, which matched her attire.

"I'd heard you'd taken up Mrs. Pickering's desperate case, but I didn't quite believe it."

Annie turned a violent shade of pink. She ducked her head, as if hoping to hide behind her neatened hair. Protectiveness washed over Katherine as she took a small step to put herself between Annie and Mrs. Fairchild's scorn.

"I have pledged to help Miss Pickering make her match, and I'm proud to do so."

Katherine didn't care to play the matchmaker at all, but for Annie's sake, she hoped she feigned exuberance well enough to fool her rival.

Mrs. Fairchild turned up her nose. "Of course you

have. It isn't as though you've been given any more respectable offers."

Was that insult meant for one of her sisters? Katherine drew herself up and balled her hands into fists to keep them from trembling. Mrs. Fairchild only undertook clients with the purest reputations, the most demure, polite, pretty girls from wealthy families. If they were beyond reproach, then Mrs. Fairchild was the first to recommend them to wealthy men to make shallow matches of convenience, and nothing more. Most likely, those involved wound up miserable.

The rival matchmaker added, "If anyone is going to make the match of the Season, it will be Miss Young." She indicated the prim, polished, young blond woman who might as well not have had any tongue or personality of her own, for she didn't say a word. She clasped her hands in front of her cream gown and let her matchmaker speak for her.

Gritting her teeth, Katherine looked the sour older woman in the eye. "If that was your aim, you've already lost. The Season ended three weeks ago. Come, Annie," she added as she turned on her heel. "Let's go below."

The young woman seemed close to tears. She hunched in on herself as she slinked down the stairs. At the bottom, Katherine pulled her aside for Mrs.

Fairchild and her charge to pass. The rival match-maker did so with an air of superiority. Miss Young displayed as much personality as her pale dress.

"Pull yourself together," Katherine commanded in an encouraging tone. "You're happy to be here, aren't you?"

Annie's chin wobbled as she tilted her head up to meet Katherine's gaze. "I haven't got a chance next to her."

Katherine scoffed. "Why not? I've seen door latches with more personality than Miss Young."

A slim smile pulled at Annie's lips. Her dimples winked in and out of sight.

"But she's beautiful."

"If Lord Northbrook looked for beauty alone, he would already have married her. Have you seen him pay her any mind at past events?" For Annie's sake, Katherine hoped the answer was no.

She let out a bated breath as Annie shook her head.

"There you are, then. Go on and mingle. Smile. Compliment the dowager on her home. Let's keep talk of insects for when the earl knows you better, yes?"

Annie nodded. She started to step toward the open sitting room door, from which light and murmured chatter spilled. She hesitated after one step. "Aren't you coming with me?"

"I'll be in the room, but you must stand on your own and not use me as a crutch." More importantly, Katherine had a list of suspects to narrow if she had any hope of catching the Pink-Ribbon Killer before the deadline. She hardened herself to Annie's glum expression and followed the young woman into the sitting room.

Stepping into the corner to better observe everyone in the room, Katherine parted from her charge. With her shoulders bowed as if to make herself invisible, Annie joined the other debutantes on the settees and chairs ringing a table laden with the tea service.

In the sea of so many young women, the Dowager Countess of Northbrook perched like a queen in front of her subjects. Her shrewd gaze, all but hidden beneath her thick eyebrows, chased young woman after young woman as she measured each prospect. Given her severe, disapproving expression, coupled with the slate-gray turban on her head, which matched her high-necked gown, Katherine had no misgivings in believing Annie's assessment of her to be correct.

If she didn't want to see her son married, why go through the trouble of hosting a house party at such a tumultuous time?

The men clustered across the room in front of the dado, which was painted in a Grecian shoreline. They sipped amber liquid from tumblers as they conversed in low voices, likely about horseflesh or hunting. Katherine wondered which of the men was Lord Northbrook and guessed that he must be the dark-haired man who said little and snuck glances between his mother and the door.

Katherine recognized an old man in his seventies who had a mane of white hair and pronounced laugh lines around his eyes as the Duke of Somerset. A few paltry murders, one of which occurred on his estate, didn't appear to have dampened his spirits.

In fact, as a buxom maid stepped closer to offer the men refills, Somerset relinquished his tumbler and took advantage of his empty hand to pinch the woman's behind. Katherine appeared to be the only one to notice the lewd gesture. The maid curtseyed and hurried about her tasks.

In his notes on the second murder, Katherine's father had described each of the guests as potential suspects. Although not all were attending Lord North-brook's affair, the notes provided her with enough information to guess at the identities of the other men.

The man with golden-brown hair and an athletic build must be Lord Mowbry, heir to a marquess.

Although he couldn't be much older than Katherine, when the others weren't looking he gathered a somber mien, like building storm clouds, which made him seem under the weight of decades. He replaced that air, the moment someone directed a comment toward him, with a ready smile. *Is he hiding a more sinister nature?*

Katherine remembered rumors of an association between Mowbry and the first victim, Miss Smythe. She wondered whether he also had an association with the second victim, Miss Rosehill, and whether the young ladies had done something that drove him to murder.

To his left stood his constant friend, Mr. Greaves. Of the same height and build as his friend, Greaves had white-blond hair that looked purposefully mussed in the frightened owl style. His smile was even wider than Mowbry's as he engaged the group in repartee.

The last man, the tallest of the lot at well over six feet, had his back turned to her. Something about him was vaguely familiar, and Katherine nibbled on her lower lip as she tried to recall whether Papa had described a man so tall. A name eluded her, and without seeing his face, she couldn't be certain of his identity. She frowned at the back of his brown-haired head. *Who was he?*

"Contemptible, wouldn't you say?"

Katherine jumped. She pressed a hand to her middle as she glanced at the middle-aged beauty who had detached from the debutantes to stand at her elbow. Apparently, Katherine wasn't as unnoticeable as she'd hoped.

Remembering her manners, not that this woman had displayed any thus far, Katherine smiled politely. "Lady Reardon, so good to see you, but I'm afraid I don't follow."

The judgmental woman tapped one finger against her arm, subtly pointing toward Somerset, who leered at a maid as she refilled his glass.

"His room is next to ours, you know. Lord Reardon couldn't make it, I'm afraid, so I've been losing sleep. Anyway, I've already heard him celebrating his arrival with the chambermaid and trying to celebrate with the housemaid, who almost tipped over that lovely bust of Cesar in the hallway between our rooms in her haste to get away! Does he have no shame?"

Katherine hoped that the woman didn't expect her to answer, for she had no personal insight on the duke. Since he wasn't a member of the Royal Society of Investigative Techniques, she rarely crossed paths with him.

Seemingly, her silence was the answer for which

Lady Reardon hoped, because the woman continued to natter on. "I tell you, he'd better not stray his gaze toward *my* daughter."

Frankly, Katherine was surprised to hear her make such a pronouncement. "He's a duke." *Isn't wealth and status what all the matchmaking mamas care about?*

The older woman turned up her nose. "Don't be lewd. He's old enough to be her grandfather."

To many, the title of duke would supersede the matter of age. Katherine held her tongue on the matter.

Lady Reardon added, "I know all men keep mistresses, but I will see that my daughter has a better man than *that*."

It was almost admirable of her, to exclude a man from the list of eligible matches because of the way she perceived he would treat his bride. However, Lady Reardon wasn't exacting enough, in Katherine's opinion.

"You're wrong. Not all men keep mistresses." After all, her brothers-in-law did not. She or her father, the two detectives in the family, would certainly know if they had.

The other woman scoffed. "How quaint of you to think so." Her gaze strayed toward the group of debutantes, and at last, her true purpose in seeking out Katherine's company became clear. "I do hope Mrs.

Pickering paid your fee up front. If you hope to find a man without a mistress for your charge, you'll be looking a long time indeed."

This was precisely the reason Katherine chose to spend more time with the Royal Society than out at *ton* events. The moment these matrons perceived a rival, they sought to cut them down.

Leaning closer, Lady Reardon added, "Perhaps you should consider Lord Somerset. He isn't good enough for *my* daughter, but your charge, I imagine, would welcome any male attention, however brief. If Mrs. Burwick is so desperate to marry off her daughter that she'd host her party so soon after... Well, I can only say there is much competition for a husband here."

Judging by the grasp Mrs. Burwick kept on her daughter's shoulder, Katherine couldn't tell whether the sharp-nosed brunette was in pain or if her face always looked so sour. Mrs. Burwick must be desperate indeed. And why *had* she hosted that party so soon after the first murder? Katherine almost felt sorry for Miss Burwick. Standing almost as tall as Katherine and with hips just as wide, she was no dainty flower.

The older woman turned away. "If you'll excuse me, I believe my daughter requires my attention."

As Lady Reardon sashayed away, the hostess

called for the gentlemen to join the ladies for a word game. Although Katherine excelled at word games and *Consequences* was one of her favorites, due to the hilarity brewed from each person adding a line to the growing narrative without knowing the previous line, she was happy to remain in the corner alone.

The gentlemen milled among the ladies as papers and pencils were handed around the circle. Katherine counted her suspects, conveniently all in one place.

Wait—where was the brown-haired fellow who towered head and shoulders above the others?

"Lady Katherine. I must admit, I didn't expect to find you here," a familiar voice said.

Katherine bit her cheek to stifle a yelp of surprise. When next she spoke with Lyle, she would ask him to develop an invention that would help with her peripheral vision. This was the second time in an hour that she's been caught unawares! As she turned to face her new companion, the breath fled her lungs. She bit back a vehement curse.

Dorian Wayland. She wondered whether her luck could wax any worse. The blighter stood with his hands clasped behind his back with military precision. Because he had commanded a company of hussars during the war against Napoleon, he did everything with both that precision and a ruthlessness that put tyrants to shame.

Katherine had had the misfortune of crossing paths with him more than once. Since returning victorious from Waterloo, he had taken up detective work for a price. As the heir of a viscount, he didn't need the money—he charged for his services on a lark.

Her father loathed him, on account of his relentless and at times merciless methods of hunting criminals. Supposedly, Wayland didn't care which ne'er-do-wells he hurt, so long as he collected his fee. If he was here, that could only mean that he meant to solve the Pink-Ribbon Murders as well, but he must be investigating under someone's employ. There was no bounty, and from what Katherine had heard, he certainly wouldn't be investigating simply to keep the streets safe.

Katherine couldn't think of profanity befitting the foul situation in which he put her. If he captured the Pink-Ribbon Killer, she wouldn't attain the independence she so desperately needed.

He dazzled her with a debonair smile that emphasized the cleft in his chin. His hazel eyes danced. "You didn't attend the last two house parties."

Although she straightened her spine as much as possible, she couldn't hope to match his height. Most men stood no taller than she did. She didn't enjoy feeling so small.

Nevertheless, she refused to show any sign of intimidation. Matching his bold gaze, she countered, "And did you?"

He chuckled. "It seems we both conducted thorough research before arriving. I take it you have the same reason as I for attending?"

"You hope to make a match between Lord Northbrook and Miss Pickering, as well?" She smiled at him sweetly.

He laughed louder, though keeping his voice to an intimate whisper. "Is that your aim? I wish you luck with it."

"I don't need luck. I have skill and years of experience."

His smile grew as he raked her with his shrewd gaze. Perhaps she shouldn't have worn the apple-green gown. With her figure, it made her resemble a pear. In fact, she'd hoped to use that fact to dissuade the gentlemen present from considering her a potential match. Now, her choice of garment seemed conspicuous and unprofessional.

"Are we still discussing matchmaking?"

She glanced at the party. They all studiously scribbled on pieces of paper before folding them and

passing them along. Annie, who seemed in good spirits, giggled at something Miss Reardon showed her
before she folded her page.

Katherine flashed Wayland another falsely sweet
smile. "What else might we be discussing?"

He cocked an eyebrow. "Are you hiding your intelligence for the benefit of these simpletons? For shame.
You're the only person worth speaking to at this
gathering."

"Is that why you've sought out my company?"

"Yes, though I will admit, I hoped you might be
willing to share information. I heard your father was
the investigator on scene at the second murder."

In fact, he had arrived after the fact, but Katherine
didn't choose to correct him. "I have no information,"
she lied.

On her right, a commotion started with a man's
yelp, followed by a gaggle of female voices.

"I do hope you're a better matchmaker than you
are a chaperone," Wayland said with a smirk. He
nodded toward the gathering.

When Katherine turned, she found Northbrook
seated with his hands in the air in surrender, a wet
pool across his breeches, and a teacup on the floor.
And Annie—what on earth? Annie patted down his
lap with a handkerchief.

Katherine didn't bother to excuse herself as she dashed away from the rival detective. *Dear me. What is Annie thinking?*

As she straightened out the matter, she struggled not to smirk. That was one way to force a match, even if it was bound to be met by some opposition.

CHAPTER FOUR

Annie balked as they reached the staircase. "I can't do it. I'll run back to London and tell Mama I feel ill."

"If you run all the way there under your own power, you likely *will* feel ill."

Given her pallor, the young woman didn't care for Katherine's joke. Annie covered her face with her hands and moaned. "How can I possibly face him after what happened this afternoon in the parlor?"

"It will be fine. You'll be in a room full of people."

Annie lifted her head. "Is that supposed to cheer me? They were all there to witness my embarrassment!"

"Perhaps next time, you ought to offer the gentleman your handkerchief so he can clean his own trousers."

Annie moaned once more into her hands.

"Come." Katherine steered her down the stairs with an arm around the shorter woman's shoulders. "Your imagination is wreaking havoc on you. I wager the guests are so far into their cups that they won't even remember the incident."

Annie brightened. "Do you think?"

Considering that over half the guests were young women hoping to catch the eye of one of the wealthy men at the party, they likely hadn't imbibed at all. However, if it would chase Annie down the stairs, Katherine would lie.

"I know. Besides, you must attend, or you'll insult the hostess. Perhaps there was a bit of a misunderstanding earlier, but it will all be forgotten by the end of the night, I promise you. Mind your glass, find your way into Lord Northbrook's company if you can, and don't turn down a dance."

On the threshold of the ballroom, Annie dug in her heels. The color faded from her cheeks once more as she surveyed the interior.

The wide room, with neoclassical pillars marching down its length to hold a second-floor balcony, was more than large enough to hold twice their number. The marble floor gleamed, with the warm light of swathes of candles glistening off a geometric pattern.

Chairs lined the wall opposite the pillar, none of them occupied. Only one of the French doors next to the chairs was open to the night air.

Annie clutched Katherine's arm. "What if no one asks me to dance?"

"Someone will ask." At least, so Katherine hoped. A proper chaperone would encourage suitors to ask, as Katherine had done for her sisters. Tonight, however, she didn't have the time to force a gentleman's hand. Her hunt for the murderer must take precedence.

The first murder had taken place after midnight during a ball on Somerset's estate, and Katherine wondered whether that meant the killer was likely to strike again tonight.

Maybe two victims were enough. Perhaps there was something in particular about Miss Smythe and Miss Rosehill that had caused their demise. Katherine dearly hoped so—though she wanted to catch the killer, she did not want it to be at the expense of another victim.

Annie asked, "Won't you keep a dance card for me? You'll let me know if someone wants to dance with me. I'll sit on the side and wait."

Katherine caught her arm as the young woman separated to do exactly that. The poor thing seemed terrified. "This is a country affair. There's no need for me to keep a dance card"—she hoped—"but you mustn't hide yourself away. Find a conversation and join it. No insects."

And leave me free to figure out which one of these guests is the killer.

Annie chewed on her lower lip as she walked into the room. She stepped on the hem of her gown and nearly stumbled into an enormous vase filled with flowers, but Katherine steered her out of harm's way.

Annie's green eyes glistened as she tilted her face up to meet Katherine's. "Won't you stay with me?"

"I'll be in the room, circulating. I promise to stop to check on you from time and time, and I'll keep an eye on you throughout." The rest of the time, she had to monitor the other guests.

Even if the room was far from its capacity, Katherine had no hope of keeping track of all of them. She had far too wide a swathe of suspects, and considered upon whom she should focus tonight.

Strangling a woman took some strength. Perhaps Katherine would contain her observations to the unmarried gentlemen in the room. That left Lords Northbrook, Mowbry, and Somerset, as well as Mr. Greaves. This left a much more manageable number, even if they would be scattered to every end of the room in pursuit of entertainment.

Blast it. She had no motive to attribute to any man in particular. *Why would someone want two young debutantes dead? Who would be next? Was it even the same killer? Would he kill again, or had the two previous deaths accomplished his goal? What if Miss Rosehill was killed by someone completely different who simply wanted to throw the investigation off by using a pink ribbon to make it* look *like the same killer?*

But if it was the same killer, and if he wasn't done, then all the women in the room were in danger. Including Annie... and possibly her. Perhaps it wouldn't be wise to let her charge get too far out of sight.

As she witnessed Lady Reardon herding her daughter away from the Duke of Somerset, Katherine pursed her lips. It was possible that Lord Somerset had turned his eye on the previous victims, who might have felt the same as Lady Reardon and refused him. Perhaps, with his wandering hands, they had even threatened to expose his lecherous ways. But whether that would anger him enough to kill was anyone's guess.

It wasn't the strongest of theories, but it was the best she had to go on for the moment.

When she stepped farther into the room, Annie clinging to her shadow, Katherine found herself intercepted by the very last man she hoped to exchange words with tonight.

"Captain Wayland."

Dressed in his hussar uniform, a midnight-blue coat with gold bars and tan trousers, he bowed over her hand. He might have chosen his military uniform tonight to remind her that he had waged a war—and won. She raised her chin mulishly. If he thought to intimidate her, he would soon discover that she wasn't easily cowed. Anyway, the race to unmask a murderer was a very different sort of war.

Annie curtseyed, and as Wayland bowed over Annie's hand, Katherine smirked. The moment he straightened, she gave him a demure smile.

His eyes narrowed, and well they should— Katherine only played demure when it suited her goal. "Captain, how kind of you to honor our discussion earlier. I'd nearly forgotten."

Her eyes widening with curiosity, Annie grew bold enough to ask, "What did you forget?"

Katherine's smile grew as the woman behind the grand piano stroked the keys in a new song. "Why, Captain Wayland has agreed to stand up as your first dance partner this evening."

Annie turned pink. "He has?" She dipped in

another curtsey, pressing her lips together until her dimples winked into sight.

Not the twitch of an eyelash betrayed Wayland's shock or distress at having been so cornered. He was a master at concealing his feelings.

After holding Katherine's gaze a moment, he turned to Annie and recovered smoothly. "Indeed. It would be my honor. I only regret leaving Lady Katherine without a partner. If you'll wait a moment, I'm certain I can convince Lord Mowbry or perhaps the host to stand up with you."

Well played. Katherine fingered the line of her bodice and wondered how was she going to get out of *this.* Although a weak excuse, she said, "How flattering, but I couldn't possibly take a partner away from the debutantes in attendance, not when the gentlemen are so outnumbered. I am here only in the capacity of a chaperone, after all."

Wayland cocked an eyebrow. "Does that mean you must deny yourself the chance for a bit of fun? Lady Katherine, I didn't know you for such a martyr."

Scoundrel.

As Katherine gathered herself to return his quip, Annie's shoulders slumped. She curled in on herself as if trying to make herself smaller. "If you'd prefer to dance with Katherine instead..."

Wayland glanced between both women. Clenching her jaw, Katherine drew herself up and met his gaze boldly. *Do the right thing, you bounder.*

He gave Annie a shallow bow. "Forgive me, it seems my conscience has spoiled the evening. I, of course, am far more eager to dance with you."

Katherine released a breath. Maybe Wayland had an honorable bone in him, after all.

As he straightened, his hazel eyes danced. "However, I don't see why I can't prove an admirable dance partner to both of you. Lady Katherine, perhaps you'll do me the honor of standing up with me for the second set. I won't take no for an answer."

Drat. Judging by the finality of his tone, he meant his threat. If she tried to avoid the dance, he would hound her for the rest of the evening. "It would be my pleasure," she said, though she meant nothing of the sort.

What game did he play by forcing her to dance with him? It could have been simply to prevent her from learning any more about the suspects present, or he might have hoped to wheedle information from her. It would be a cold day indeed before she shared her knowledge with *him*.

As Wayland liberated her from Annie's presence,

Katherine struck out around the perimeter of the room to find her suspects.

Lord Mowbry didn't need watching, given that he was already under the admiring eyes of at least six women, not all of them debutantes. With Mr. Greaves at his side, exuding every bit as much charm, Lord Mowbry entertained his companions, who giggled and sighed at his conversational prowess. Katherine rolled her eyes and continued walking. Annie and Wayland could only occupy each other for so long.

Mrs. Burwick whispered to her prim-faced daughter as she herded her past Katherine toward the young lord, "He just lost his fiancée. He'll want to fill that void as soon as possible, and you *must* catch his eye."

Katherine paused, but by the time she turned, the Burwicks had stepped out of earshot. *Who has lost his fiancée? Was one of the murder victims engaged?* It could have been that Mrs. Burwick meant the matter in a figurative sense and that the mystery woman had called off the engagement.

She nearly pursued the pair in an attempt to learn more, but movement near the door to the garden caught her eye. Lord Northbrook was attempting to lead Miss Young outside!

Katherine's heart skipped a beat. The blood roared in her ears as she quickened her step. With the Season cut short, this party was the killer's only opportunity to kill again, which could be why Northbrook was hosting the party—to kill again. Katherine must prevent Miss Young from venturing out-of-doors with him at all costs.

She intercepted the pair moments before they stepped out into the cool night air and planted herself in their path. "Lord Northbrook," she said with a sunny smile and small curtsey. "I don't believe I've thanked you properly for throwing this gallant affair. It is most diverting from the ennui in London."

The young earl stiffened. "You should direct your compliments to my mother. It is all her doing, I assure you."

From the way he darted glances over her shoulder at the garden, she could tell he wanted desperately to escape. Unfortunately, Katherine couldn't let him. Although she had no evidence to point to Northbrook as the Pink-Ribbon Killer, Katherine couldn't take the chance. Even if it wasn't him, someone else might be lurking in the gardens in wait.

"Are you taking a turn about the gardens? I'll join you. I could use some fresh air, and it looks as though you've lost your chaperone, Miss Young."

The young woman's cheeks turned pink, and she

took a small step back. Northbrook didn't appear to notice, but he also seemed reluctant to accept Katherine's company. Given the wistful look on his face, he would rather escape into the garden without either of them.

"Lady Katherine."

Katherine pinned her smile in place as Mrs. Fairchild's bitter voice rang through the air. It appeared that Miss Young's chaperone wasn't far, after all. Katherine turned to face the cutting woman.

Her mouth fixed in a sour moue, Mrs. Fairchild threaded her arm through Katherine's. "Let's not interrupt the young, shall we? I'm certain Lord Northbrook and Miss Young would prefer to continue their stroll around the room without two old matrons like you and me darkening their fun."

Katherine was closer in age to Miss Young, whom she guessed to be near twenty years old, than she was to Mrs. Fairchild's thirty-five years. Neither of them was old in any way, and Northbrook rested squarely between them in terms of age. As the matchmaker tried to lead her away, Katherine dug in her heels and used her superior height to her advantage.

"A stroll around the room, you say? I believe the pair intended to go out into the garden."

Miss Young flushed crimson. She curtsied to the

earl and mumbled an excuse about not feeling well and needing to sit a moment. If she used the trick to buy herself a few more moments alone with the object of her affections, it didn't work in her favor. The moment he deposited her in the line of chairs, he departed, likely with the guise of fetching a glass of lemonade for her.

With a grip like a dog's jaws on a bone, Mrs. Fairchild led Katherine across the room to the shadow of one of the pillars. The moment they stood in shadow, she dropped Katherine's arm. Katherine surreptitiously flexed her fingers, which tingled from lack of circulation.

The pianist ended her song. The hairs rose on the back of Katherine's neck. She had to extract herself from Mrs. Fairchild soon. If she remained here, Wayland would surely find her and claim the dance he'd threatened.

The shorter woman wagged her finger in Katherine's face. "Don't think I haven't guessed your aim."

"I beg your pardon?"

Mrs. Fairchild harrumphed. "You're trying to undermine me! Well, I've news for you, *Lady* Katherine. Preventing Lord Northbrook from marrying my client will not earn an engagement to yours. She's beyond help!"

On instinct, Katherine scanned the crowd, searching for Annie. She didn't spot her or Wayland, with his noticeable height. She didn't know whether to be relieved or wary. "I'm not trying to undermine you." Katherine tried to curb the bite in her voice, to no avail. From the corner of her eye, she noticed Lord Somerset slipping out into the gardens. *What reason could he have for venturing out there alone?* She had to follow him.

Unfortunately, Mrs. Fairchild stood in her way. Judging by her mulish, scathing expression, she wouldn't let Katherine pass easily.

Perhaps she would drop the matter if she knew the truth. "I wasn't trying to undermine you. I had Miss Young's best interests at heart—"

The shrewish woman cut her off as she was attempting to explain her efforts to preserve Miss Young's life. "*You* aren't her matchmaker. Perhaps you ought to leave concern for her best interests to me."

Sarding stubborn woman! Katherine bit her tongue. She stole a quick glance toward the door, but Somerset was already out of sight. "Believe what you will," Katherine said sharply.

A glass shattered, providing her with the distraction she needed to leave unimpeded. She heartily hoped the spilled drink wasn't at Annie's hands again.

If it was, she'd never convince the young woman to return to the gathering.

Men and women craned their necks, hoping to see the cause of the disturbance. None of them glanced at Katherine as she briskly strode the length of the ballroom and exited into the cool air.

Only a sliver of light drifted from the crescent moon. A few sparse lanterns at the junction of paths provided a meager measure of illumination by which to see.

She hurried along, her eyes barely making out the shapes of the path and the bushes in the dim light. She stepped lightly to avoid making sound as she searched for Somerset.

A woman's girlish giggle wafted from her right. Katherine hoped Miss Young wasn't out in the garden. She crept onward and took the next path leading to her right.

In the swathe of shadows, she found a grotesque figure. It took her a moment, with the spots from the lantern still glowing in her field of view, for her to realize that it was not one figure but two, locked in an amorous embrace. Crouching nearer to a bush to keep herself hidden, Katherine tiptoed forward.

She couldn't be certain of the woman's identity, but the scant light of the moon glinted silver off the strands of the man's hair—Somerset. He fumbled over the woman's breasts with his left hand as he kissed her. The right was tucked up against his body. His ineptitude seemed to be frustrating them both. Not that Katherine would want him pawing at her to begin with, but she wondered why he didn't use his right hand.

Come to think of it, he hadn't used his right hand at all this afternoon. He'd held the tumbler in his right hand, but always shifted it to the left before handing it to a maid or taking a sip. Was there a reason for it—an injury, perhaps?

Katherine shifted, hoping to find a better position to spy on Somerset. Although she hoped the encounter wouldn't progress past kissing and pawing, she couldn't leave a defenseless woman in his care. If she left and the woman became the next murder victim, she'd never forgive herself.

Crunch. Katherine's slipper landed on the gravel. The couple broke apart.

"What was that?"

Katherine recognized the voice from earlier as belonging to a spinster chaperoning her cousin to the event.

"Nothing, love. You're hearing things."

The Duke of Somerset reached for the spinster

again, but she shook him off. "It is not my imagination. Someone's out there. We'll be found."

Somerset seemed reluctant to end the interlude, but the spinster was adamant. Within seconds, they retreated down the path away from Katherine. When they reached the next junction, they parted ways.

Katherine let out an exasperated breath. What a waste of time. She was turning back down the path, prepared to return to the gathering, when a woman's shriek split the air.

CHAPTER FIVE

Katherine's heart lodged in her throat. She bolted toward the sound.

Ahead, a man's silhouette came from a side path and crossed in front of one of the lanterns, but he was there and gone before she discerned any identifiable traits. Phil's advice to catch him in the act and force a confession rang in her head. This was her chance to apprehend the killer!

She tripped over a loose stone and landed on one knee. Hissing in pain, she forced herself upright and in hot pursuit of the culprit.

The path forked ahead, and she wondered which way he had gone. No one else was about, and Katherine realized he had run away from the shriek. As much as she hungered to catch the blackguard, if he'd left a woman injured, she should stop to help.

Katherine turned and hurried toward the direction of the sound instead.

As she stumbled past another lantern, she found Annie, alone and unharmed. Pausing to catch her breath, she asked, "Did you hear a scream?"

The light glinted off Annie's wide eyes. "Oh, forgive me, that was me. I was so excited, I couldn't contain myself."

Katherine blinked, not quite soaking in the young woman's words. She had shrieked from excitement of... being out in the garden.

Annie held out her cupped hands, opening them enough for Katherine to peer inside. Two fuzzy antennae peeked out from between her thumbs. "It's a violet-banded elephant moth. I've never seen one before!"

Distant footsteps crunched on the gravel.

"Let it be," Katherine whispered to her charge. "We must return inside at once before someone notices our absence. We can't have the whole party knowing that you were out here alone."

And never mind what she'd been doing alone. Somehow Katherine didn't think that collecting insects was going to help Annie's chances of landing a husband.

Annie blinked her owlish eyes. Strands of her hair

had worked free of her coiffure, half-covering her face again. "Didn't you hear me? It's extremely rare. I must keep it for my collection!"

If ever Katherine found herself in the position of chaperone again, she would make doubly certain before accepting the job that the young woman in question was not unreasonably fond of insects.

A man called, "Is someone hurt?"

They must have heard Annie scream from inside the house, but she couldn't let them know *why* she'd screamed.

Thinking quickly, Katherine shouted, "Yes. Over here!"

Inwardly cringing, she held out her hands to Annie and said, "Give it here, and sit on the ground. Follow my lead."

Her voice must have held some semblance of authority, for Annie obeyed at once. As Katherine cupped her hands around the moth, its legs tickled her palm. She fought back a shudder.

From the ground, Annie asked, "Why am I sitting?"

The footsteps thundered closer.

The insect did more tickling.

Katherine lowered her voice, not certain if her words carried over the sound. "Hold your ankle as if hurts. Say nothing if you can help it. I'll do the talking."

The men arrived first. Lords Northbrook and Mowbry, with Mr. Greaves a few paces behind, and —*tarnation!*—Captain Wayland. As Mr. Greaves came apace of Lord Mowbry, he clapped a hand on his friend's shoulder.

"There you are, old friend. You had me worried."

"You think I scream like a girl?"

Wait. They'd been together when Katherine had departed the ballroom, which made her wonder why Greaves would be worried.

But she didn't have time to ponder the question, for Wayland stepped forward with an air of authority. "What happened?"

Lord Northbrook glared at him then took a step forward and crouched beside Annie. "Did someone harm you?" His voice was gentler than the captain's.

Annie looked from the host to Katherine. Her chest remained still, as if she feared to so much as breathe without permission.

Katherine forced a smile. "No—oh!" She made an involuntary hoot as the moth between her palms shifted its wings. *Vile creature.* She tried not to show her distaste or desire to hurry everyone along. "I'm afraid Miss Pickering has turned her ankle. She has no one to blame but herself."

Northbrook squinted at the lantern. "Perhaps we ought to put out more lamps."

The women arrived, flushed and harried from the run. Curiosity ran rampant over their features as they craned their necks to peer around the men. The Dowager Countess of Northbrook pushed to the front of the group, clasping her hands in front of her as she strode serenely. Katherine tried to emulate her stance, hoping no one would notice the bizarre way she held her hand.

Wayland paid entirely too much notice to her.

The light cut across the hostess's face, making her look even more formidable. "What has happened here?" she demanded.

Katherine yelped as the moth moved again. "Ah—I beg your forgiveness, Lady Northbrook." *Stop it,* she thought to the excitable insect. "Miss Pickering turned her ankle. If someone will be so kind as to render his assist—ah!—ance, we'll re—ee!—tire at once to ensure she gets her rest."

Be still, or I will squish you. Annie might have some sort of attachment to this vermin, but Katherine most certainly did not.

She fought not to squirm as the hostess pinned her

beneath a disapproving stare, which was a difficult task when the moth's legs tickled her palm. *Do moths bite?*

"I'll gladly volunteer my arm," Lord Northbrook said. "It seems only fair, seeing as it was my garden that so injured her."

Katherine smiled. *Fantastic!* Not only had she managed to hide Annie's predilection for insect collecting, but she'd wrangled Northbrook into noticing the young woman. Who said Katherine couldn't solve a mystery and perform her matchmaking duties at the same time?

Her smile faded as Wayland stepped forward. "Allow me to help, as well."

Katherine glared at him. They needed only one man to carry Annie. Surely Lord Northbrook could handle that task on his own. He seemed to be sturdily built.

The hostess herded away the guests with a biting reprimand over paying too much attention to a moment of disgrace. Annie's face flushed, and she hid behind her hair.

"Come now, Miss Pickering," Wayland said as he crossed to her side, opposite Northbrook. "Are you able to stand, or will we have to carry you?"

Poor Annie tried to shrink into herself. From

beneath a fringe of her hair, she glared at Katherine as though blaming her for the situation.

All would be forgiven the moment Katherine returned the moth intact, she was sure.

"I can stand," Annie answered, her voice small.

Wayland directed Northbrook to take hold of Annie's opposite arm and help her to rise. When they did, the silly woman didn't even have the sense to lean more of her weight on Northbrook.

Instead, she leaned heavily into Wayland. Katherine tried to catch her eye and surreptitiously jerk her head toward Northbrook, but Annie didn't appear to notice. Judging by his ill-concealed smirk as he helped Annie to turn toward the nearest door, Wayland did notice.

A tortoise would have won a race against the procession. Katherine followed, biting her cheek to keep from making a sound as the moth made a bid for freedom through the crack of her fingers. It wasn't in danger of escaping, but the sensation made her squirm. She tried to cup her hands to give the two-inch-wide insect more room, but it didn't help at all. When Wayland glanced over his shoulder before turning sideways to help Annie through a door, Katherine froze.

"Are you all right, Lady Katherine?" called Wayland.

She fought not to grimace. "Yes. I stepped wrong, is all."

If this insect didn't behave, she would feed it to her dog.

"Oh dear," Wayland said, his tone liberally laced with amusement. "Do watch where you're stepping, or we might have to carry you in after Miss Pickering."

"I'm certain Lady Katherine can manage quite well on her own," Northbrook interjected.

Katherine entered behind him and shut the door, waiting for her eyes to adjust. Light filtered through from farther in the manor, but not near this particular entrance. "Thank you, Lord Northbrook. I can."

Wayland laughed despite the tension in the air directed toward him. "I never meant to imply she could not. But you must admit, today has held ill luck when it comes to matters of grace."

Annie emitted a low noise that resembled a moan or whimper.

"Are you in pain?" Northbrook asked.

Likely so, but of an emotional sort rather than physical. Katherine kept the thought to herself, hoping not to remind either of past embarrassments.

When Annie shook her head, mute, Northbrook

told Wayland, "Perhaps it would be better if I carried her."

"Nonsense," Wayland answered. "I insist on helping."

Surely, he didn't think to ingratiate himself to Annie in order to glean Katherine's father's findings regarding the murders. Those, she refused to share. She needed whatever advantage she could find.

The moth beat its wings again. Katherine bit her tongue to stifle a yelp. She'd forgotten it was there for a moment, her hands growing slack.

Lud, don't let it escape now!

The procession reached a wide staircase. "Are you able to brave the stairs?" Northbrook asked.

Annie nodded, her face pointed toward the ground. "Yes. I'm feeling much improved. I could likely manage on my own."

Katherine was almost inclined to let her, if it meant ridding them of Wayland's company.

Unfortunately, Northbrook insisted on seeing her directly to her door. Katherine had half a mind to slip past them and let the moth free, but she held herself in check. After what felt like an eternity of beating insect wings and the touch of spider-thin legs, they reached the top of the stairs. Katherine directed them down the corridor to Annie's room.

Something long and thin probed between her fingers. It peeked through the crack into the open air, growing longer. An inch. Two inches.

Please tell me that is not the moth's man-part. She had to set this thing free posthaste, before something even more distasteful happened.

Clutching her hands to her belly and hoping to hide the protrusion, Katherine said faintly, "I think Miss Pickering and I can handle ourselves quite well from here."

"We've only a few more steps," Wayland answered cheerfully. "This is the door, isn't it?"

Thank Jove, it was. "Yes."

As he reached for the latch to the door, Katherine recalled the collection of dead insects Annie had strewn around the room. She opened her mouth, but it was too late. The door swung inward. She cringed.

The men didn't say a word as they helped Annie inside and deposited her on the stool to the vanity. A candle glowed by the bedside. The door to the adjoining room was open, and Emma dashed inside with a happy yip. She paused to sniff the boots of the gentlemen.

Nowhere did Katherine spot a single insect. *Bless you, Harriet.*

As if summoned by her thoughts, her maid

appeared in the doorway and snapped her fingers. "Don't disturb the gentlemen, Emma." She glanced from Katherine to the men. "Is something amiss? Did you need anything, Lady Katherine?"

"Not at the moment, thank you. The gentlemen were helping Miss Pickering up the stairs. She turned her ankle."

"Oh. I have a tea that will help with that."

Harriet had a tea for every situation. Katherine held her tongue as her maid disappeared once more. *Oh dear.* She pitied Annie. Harriet's noxious teas were rarely palatable.

Lord Northbrook frowned. "Is tea appropriate for this situation?"

Katherine grinned. "Tea is appropriate for any situation. Thank you for your assistance, both of you."

Northbrook inclined his head. "It was my pleasure. I wish you ladies a good night. Miss Pickering, if that ankle gives you grief and you'd like to call a physician, let my housekeeper know at once, and we'll send for one."

Annie tucked her feet behind her and mumbled her thanks.

Northbrook stared at Katherine for a moment, and she feared that the sarding protrusion was visible. The moth had stopped moving for the moment, but in a way, that made the situation even worse, because she wondered what it was doing in there. She smiled and tucked her hands tighter to her body.

Although Northbrook took a step toward the door, Wayland did not. He knelt and offered his hand for Emma, who wore a jonquil-yellow ribbon, to sniff instead. "And who is this captivating creature?"

Northbrook lost interest in the conversation and departed.

"That is Emma, my dog," Katherine informed him. "Be careful. She's a little thief."

Wayland laughed. He told the pug, "I catch thieves and lock them in cages, I'll have you know."

Not intelligent enough to recognize a threat when she heard one, Emma balanced on her hind legs and begged for his attention. He obliged, scratching her beneath her ribbon, where she loved most. One of her back legs thumped the ground, and she lost her balance.

Laughing again as the dog fell to the floor, Wayland straightened. "Oh dear. She's swooned."

"Yes," Katherine bit off. "I imagine you have that effect on multiple women. Allow me to show you out."

He pinned her beneath a debonair smile. "What a shame you seem to be beyond my charms."

Annie's eyes grew wide and she watched them with rapt attention.

"Quite." Katherine gestured to the door with her chin. She herded Wayland out of the room, but he didn't move past the threshold to the door.

Lowering his voice, he vowed, "I'm not leaving until I get a glimpse of what you're carrying. You've been cradling it as though it's your newborn babe. Is it a clue?"

Katherine battled the urge to toss the moth down the neck of his shirt and tell him he was welcome to it. Instead, she took a step back and told him, "Whatever it is, it's *my* business, not yours." She swung the door closed with her hips. One benefit to having a wide figure. She smirked.

Turning, she rested her back against the door and held out her hands to Annie. "Take this *thing* away from me. It's... *doing* something."

Annie approached, her eyes wide. Enthusiasm crossed her face as she bent to examine the protuberance. "That's its proboscis!"

It sounded revolting. Katherine didn't respond.

Grinning, Annie straightened, her dimples winking. "It must think you taste like a flower."

"Take it, or I'm throwing it out the window."

Annie's smile shrank as she accepted the moth,

cradling it to her chest as she mumbled about finding a jar of some kind to house it. Harriet could help her with that once she returned with tea. Katherine refused to spend another second in close proximity to that disgusting creature.

She wiped her palms on her dress, but it wasn't enough. Detouring to her bedchamber, she cleaned her hands in a basin along the wall. She still felt the insect's legs tickling her skin.

A portable lamp rested unlit on the bedside table. After finding a tinderbox, Katherine lit the lamp and called through the adjoining doorway. "I'm going back into the garden. Watch Emma for me, will you?"

"Wait," Annie squeaked. "What if she—"

Whatever the end of that sentence was, Katherine didn't wait to hear it. In fact, she hoped it would happen. It still wouldn't be just recompense for carrying that moth for so long.

As she retraced her steps, Katherine met with none of the guests. The revelry must have been continuing in the ballroom, given the faint sounds of music and laughter wafting through the manor. She exited into the garden unimpeded.

She hurried to the spot where she'd found Annie. Once there, she slowed as she continued along the path. She bent, holding the lamp lower to illuminate the ground. The figure that she'd seen but been unable to pursue must have left some sort of trace behind.

When Annie had screamed, everyone had come running to see to her well-being. Was the killer among them, or had he beaten a hasty retreat into the house, afraid to come outside and show himself?

If Annie had unknowingly been in danger, her scream might have chased off the murderer before he had a chance to grab her, or she might simply have scared someone out for a walk—or an illicit tryst—in the garden. It was possible the man Katherine chased wasn't even the murderer.

Katherine resolved to keep a much closer eye on her charge from then on. What she really wanted, however, was to find a clue that might lead to the apprehension of the criminal.

At the junction where she'd spotted the man, she found just such a clue, a boot print in the softer dirt next to the gravel walk. Oh, if only she'd had the swift-hardening plaster Lyle used to take shoe impressions! When he'd offered her a container, it had seemed too cumbersome to fit in her reticule.

Even if she couldn't match the exact boot, given the dampness in the air that hailed rain overnight, Katherine could do the next best thing. She fished a long string from her reticule. Knotting it once, she placed the ball on the tip of the toe. She drew the string in a straight line until she reached the heel, where she knotted the thread again.

Grinning, she lifted the string to examine her handiwork. Now, all she had to do was match the length of the string to a man's boot, and she would have her suspect.

CHAPTER SIX

The task of measuring men's boots to find the culprit would have been worlds easier had Katherine been able to sneak into their rooms while they were away.

Unfortunately, she had her duties as Annie's chaperone. After the scare last night, she didn't trust Annie on her own, not even in a room full of guests. There was no telling when the young woman might wander off in pursuit of a ladybug.

As it turned out, measuring men's boots while they continued to wear them was not only challenging, but it drew an unfortunate amount of unwanted attention.

Throughout the next morning and into the afternoon, Katherine developed a habit of dropping small objects on the floor, and quickly laying out her thread as she bent over to retrieve them. The entire gathering likely thought her the clumsiest woman ever to live. Unfortunately, she most often found herself standing next to one of the married men who hadn't been on her suspect list.

She'd confirmed that none of them had the proper sized feet to have been lurking in the garden yesterday, though one or two came close at just a touch bigger or smaller, enough that they might match if the impression left by the boot had been smudged. Every time a man stepped into her peripheral vision, she arranged to drop something and take his measurements.

Unfortunately, she couldn't convince Annie to interact with any of the eligible men. Out of mortification, the young woman had retreated into herself and seemed determined to act the mouse and cling to the nearest debutante's shadow.

Nevertheless, Katherine had once managed to find herself next to Lord Northbrook, whose feet were too large for the boot print. She accidentally took Wayland's measurements at least six times, and they were also too large.

As a man stepped next to her position behind the parlor settee, she dropped the handkerchief wadded in her hand and bent to retrieve it. In her other palm resided the knotted string. She inwardly groaned as she recognized those Hessian boots.

When she straightened, Wayland smirked. His eyes danced. "If you're wondering whether they're proportionate, you only have to ask."

Her cheeks flamed. She fanned herself with her hand, forgetting for a moment that she held her handkerchief. The fabric fluttered in a small flag of surrender, drawing the eye.

Surreptitiously, she stepped back to hide herself behind Wayland's large form as the conversation turned to the weather of late, cool and cloudy. But today the sun peeked through the clouds now and again, giving the illusion of summer.

"You're despicable. That is a far from appropriate topic to discuss with a lady."

At her hissed chastisement, his smile grew. "Should the lady understand the reference?" he quipped.

She had married sisters, a curious mind, and access to a great deal of books. Nevertheless, she didn't deign to answer his comment as she waited for her cheeks to cool.

He persisted. "I don't believe examining men's feet is appropriate for a lady, either."

Katherine glared at him and stuffed her handkerchief into her bodice.

He leaned closer, lowering his head to murmur in

her ear. The other guests appeared rapt to a tale Lord Mowbry was telling about hunting or horse racing. For once, no one glanced in Katherine's direction, and Annie still seemed out of sorts but contained in her corner of the settee.

"You found a clue. I know you did. And evidently it has something to do with a man's foot. If you're searching for evidence of mud or some such, need I remind you that most will have brought a change of footwear for every day? Explain to me what you're looking for, and I can help you search, likely far less conspicuously."

Katherine balled her fists and took a step away. "I will never join forces with you," she vowed, her voice little more than a whisper. She found Wayland and his tactics irritating, but that wasn't the main reason. If her father thought Wayland had helped her solve the case, he might not give her the dowry, and she needed that for her independence.

He cocked an eyebrow. "That's what they told me in the war. Eventually, they all surrendered."

She turned to face him. "I won't *surrender,* and you've only proved my point."

"And what might that be?"

"That you have no morals and no limitations. There is a right and a wrong way to do things—"

One side of his mouth curved up in a half-smirk, but his eyes held dead-serious conviction. "There is a right and a wrong way to catch a murderer? Lady Katherine, please tell me, is there anything you wouldn't do to ensure that another helpless young woman doesn't fall prey to this fiend?"

She glowered at him. In this case, he might be right. As loath as she was to admit it, she would do anything to solve this case and earn her independence. Anything except this. "I won't work with you."

"I thought you wanted to solve this murder investigation."

Although they spoke in low voices that likely didn't carry over the lively conversation mere feet away, she lowered her voice further. "I do. And I will, but I'll do it on my own merit."

"Odd, that you'd proclaim such. The only words to emerge from that pretty mouth of yours this afternoon have been your father's."

Pretty mouth? Katherine seethed. Had they been alone in the room, she likely would have done something she would regret, such as slap him.

No, she doubted she would regret that at all.

A tendril of the others' conversation caught her ear and her attention. She stepped closer to the settee behind Annie and inserted herself. "Bowl and nine pins? That sounds like a splendid idea on such a fine day." She would take any excuse to remove herself from Wayland's company, even for a moment.

Her enthusiasm for the idea was soon echoed around the room, and Katherine excused herself to fetch her bonnet. While she was above with Annie, she collected her dog. Although dropping various items had seemed ingenious when she'd begun, she was through feeling like a lummox. Better she pretend to pet Emma.

The pug led her through the manor, eager to be outdoors, but Annie balked by the exit. She looked up at Katherine, her eyes pleading. She wore the same sea-green day dress as yesterday, paired with a white shawl to make it appear less likely to attract attention. If Katherine noticed the garment, others undoubtedly would as well, but Annie hadn't brought many clothes. Katherine suspected she didn't own many. "Perhaps I'll return to my room and tend to the moth," Annie said. Harriet had found a jar for the blasted insect, and it was now more pampered than Emma. "You can make my excuses. Tell them I have a headache."

Katherine drew herself up. "I will do no such thing. You've had a fabulous morning."

"I haven't said a word. I've been afraid to breathe."

Emma whined and tried to tug Katherine into the

garden. She used all two stone of her weight. Katherine bent and tucked her pet beneath her arm, much to the pug's dismay. "No one has said a word about the events of yesterday."

Annie's cheeks turned pink. "Lord Northbrook asked after my ankle."

"You see? He is concerned for your health."

"He was only being polite. He hasn't acknowledged me, otherwise."

Steering the shorter woman outside with an arm around her shoulders, Katherine said, "Let's rectify that, shall we? Are you any good at lawn bowling?"

Annie studied her shoes. "I've been told I have a strong arm."

Katherine smiled. "There we are, then. You'll impress him during the game, I'm certain of it. Hurry now, before they begin without you."

Annie nibbled on her lower lip. "Don't you intend to play?"

Setting her eager dog back on the ground and straightening the jaunty green ribbon tied to her collar, Katherine answered, "I have Emma to look after. We'll have fun watching, I'm certain."

Reluctantly, Annie parted from her to rejoin the procession on the lawn. Katherine strolled with Emma, touring a neglected corner of the estate until the dog finished her business. Once Katherine was certain she wouldn't make a mess in front of the guests, she led her pet closer.

Lord Somerset, Lord Mowbry, and Mr. Greaves were her targets, after measuring the string against most of the other men at the gathering. For the moment, Katherine didn't spot Captain Wayland. For that, she could only be relieved.

Emma, for her part, was only too eager to make everyone's acquaintance. She soon drew the admiring eye of every lady at the gathering, and earned several words of praise as she shamelessly begged for attention.

Lord Mowbry must not have been pleased at no longer being surrounded by beautiful women, because he soon waded into the throng to introduce himself to Katherine's pet.

Emma yipped as he came near. She bolted behind Katherine's skirt, dragging the leash around her ankles.

"Emma, what's possessed you?" Katherine yelped as the leash pulled taut and she lost her balance. As she pitched forward into Lord Mowbry, her hand slackened around the leash, and Emma broke free. Katherine braced her hands against Mowbry to soften her fall, but he tumbled to the ground with her. The impact jolted her. As gasps and exclamations resounded, she started to rise. Her hand brushed his boot top.

"Terribly sorry, my lord. Please forgive my clumsiness." Katherine played the demure, bacon-brained lady as she used one hand to uncurl the knotted string in her palm. While she was so close to him, she must at all costs measure his boot.

"Think nothing of it, Lady Katherine, but please, I beg you—rise."

Katherine pretended to push herself up, but let her arm tremble. She collapsed across his legs this time. "Oh, dear. I think I've hurt my wrist."

"Allow me to offer my assistance."

Goodness! Go away, Northbrook.

"Yes, allow me to assist, Lady Katherine."

Lud, not Wayland too.

When Wayland spoke, the ring of people parted for him to pass. He managed to plant himself in Northbrook's path without seeming to do it intentionally. Was he helping her?

Katherine laid out the string next to Mowbry's boot. Sard it all, if he would only stop moving, she could check his foot!

Annie stepped forward, well meaning, and reached out her hands as if to help Katherine rise. *No.*

Leave! She almost had the measurement, despite Lord Mowbry's squirming and grumbling.

Emma barked as she dashed forward, twining around Annie's ankles like a cat. With a yelp, Annie lost her balance as well. For a moment, Katherine feared she would fall on the pile.

She fell into Lord Northbrook instead. At least he was occupied for the moment, and Wayland busied himself putting the pair to rights.

Mowbry's boot lined up with the knots on her string in a perfect match. Katherine's heart skipped a beat, and the blood roared in her ears. Mowbry had been lurking in the garden. She remembered Mrs. Burwick mentioning something about one of the eligible men losing his fiancée, and she'd heard rumors connecting Mowbry and one of the victims. Had he been involved with—and possibly killed—two women? This was hardly damning evidence, but it was a start.

With a less than polite expression, Lord Mowbry got to his feet, as Wayland clung to Katherine's elbow and helped her to rise. Weakly, she apologized again for her clumsiness. She found her dog and bent to grab the leash.

When she straightened, Wayland remained indecently close. His eyes gleamed. "You found something."

Yes, but something that she would most certainly not be sharing with him. Upon excusing herself, she hurried to tug her pet closer to Annie.

The young woman looked close to tears. Her face was as red as a cherry, which camouflaged her freckles. She tried in vain to hide behind a fringe of hair that was neatly tucked onto her head. "I want to leave," she mouthed. If she used her voice, it didn't carry as far as Katherine's ears.

She put her arm around Annie's shoulders and steered her closer to the playing field once more. "If you do, you will certainly be the subject of gossip. This was all Emma's fault—she tripped me, as well. Don't let them conjure reasons for the accident that don't exist. You did nothing wrong."

Although the game resumed and Annie agreed to stay for the duration to preserve her reputation, she seemed to shrink in embarrassment. Her tosses toward the pins were weak and earned her few points and even less praise. For once, Wayland kept his distance. He ensconced himself at the sides of Lord Mowbry and Mr. Greaves, though his gaze continued to turn toward Katherine.

She ignored him as best she could, while using the other chaperones as a barrier between them. She found herself standing next to Mrs. Burwick and Lady

Reardon. As Mrs. Burwick's aloof daughter hefted the ball to take her turn, the gray-haired woman drew herself up. She cleared her throat loudly, thrusting back her shoulders and giving a pointed glance toward Lord Mowbry and Mr. Greaves.

Miss Burwick's expression soured further, but she improved her posture as she stepped forward to take her shot. None of the men seemed at all interested in the outcome of her game.

Lady Reardon chuckled. "Perhaps you'd have better luck if you arranged for Prudence to fall on top of him. Lady Katherine, might we borrow your dog?"

Katherine accepted the snide remark with poise. "You're welcome to her, but I warn you, Lord Mowbry isn't at all in the mood to look graciously upon anyone who crosses him." She searched the expressions of the two women for any signs that they recognized a sinister streak in the man. Katherine had to know more about him and his past with the two victims, and whether there was there a connection.

"Nonsense," Mrs. Burwick said. Her bearing was as stiff as her voice. She never took her eyes off her daughter. "He's grieving. You must make some allowances."

Katherine raised her eyebrows. Emma whined and pawed at her, asking for attention. She lifted her dog and scratched her while pursuing the conversation. "Forgive me, but he doesn't appear to be grieving at all. He's always smiling at the bevy of women around him."

"He's polite," Mrs. Burwick answered, snipping off her words. The shrewish expression in her eyes dared Katherine to contradict her.

She turned to Lady Reardon instead. "What say you? Is he polite but grieving?"

For all that she had been willing to disparage a duke, the matchmaking mama seemed much less keen to speak a poor word of Lord Mowbry. Hesitantly, she answered, "He did seem rather distraught when poor Miss Smythe was found."

So the rumors were true. "He cared for her, did he?"

"*Cared* for her?" The stinging voice travelled down Katherine's spine as Mrs. Fairchild joined them. She almost seemed to be gloating. If Miss Young had been given an offer already, it certainly wasn't from Lord Northbrook—he stood with his mother as he awaited his turn in the game.

With a thin smile that served as little more than a veneer atop her hostility, Mrs. Fairchild added, "I have it on good authority that he asked her to marry him right before she died."

"She declined?" That would give him motive.

"Gracious, no!" The matchmaker fluttered her hand over her chest. "What woman in her right mind would turn down the heir to a marquis? Aside from your client, that is."

Annie threw another shot toward the pins. This one barreled down the lawn but utterly missed the target. Instead, the ball rolled twenty feet long and lodged in a rosebush.

Mrs. Fairchild scoffed. "Not that Miss Pickering will be getting an offer any time soon."

Katherine wanted to defend Annie, but she didn't have time. She needed to learn more about Lord Mowbry. "What makes you believe that Lord Mowbry is in a fit state to make a proposal to anyone? Like you said, his betrothed was murdered."

"If he's proposed once, he's looking for a wife. It won't be terribly hard to bring him up to snuff again," Mrs. Fairchild said.

Unless he'd had genuine feelings for Miss Smythe, but if he'd killed her, one had to wonder how deep those feelings could be. A murder of passion might make sense, especially if she'd turned him down, but that didn't explain the death of Miss Rosehill. Perhaps had he rebounded quickly, as Mrs. Fairchild had suggested, and asked Miss Rosehill to marry him, too.

It seemed unlikely that two women would reject him, however.

Mrs. Burwick lifted her chin, validated. "Precisely. He has a hole in his life that only a wife can fill."

"How do you know this?" Katherine asked. "Did he propose to Miss Rosehill, as well?"

"Don't be daft," Mrs. Fairchild snapped. "He paid no more attention to her than he did to any other debutante at the party. Not a woman with so poor family connections as she."

Lady Reardon pointed across the lawn. "Oh dear, Lady Katherine. It looks as though you should tend to your charge." Her voice was thick with amusement.

Annie crouched on all fours, her bottom wiggling as she tried to fish the ball from beneath the rosebush without finding herself scoured by the thorns. Katherine took the opportunity to leave. To be honest, she was glad to be rid of those busybodies, even if they had provided vital information about her main suspect in the pink-ribbon murders. If Lord Mowbry murdered his fiancée, she would need to find a way to prove it.

CHAPTER SEVEN

"I was thinking," Katherine said. "Maybe Miss Smythe's death was an accident. Maybe Miss Rosehill was the intended victim all along. By all accounts, their appearance was similar. Do you think the murderer intended to kill her the first time but chose the wrong target? It would have been dark in the garden."

Harriet laid the ivory-backed brush on the vanity and pulled the hairpins out of her mouth. "Stop twisting. I can hear you well enough if you face forward."

"Harriet," Katherine lamented, drawing out her maid's name as she capitulated. She wanted her friend's opinion on the theory.

Once she retrieved the brush, Harriet tapped it on Katherine's shoulder. "You're speculating."

"That's what detective work is—speculation based

on the facts." Once Katherine had a sound theory, she could discern the best method of pursuing it. It didn't make sense that Mowbry would kill Miss Smythe given that he'd asked for her hand, but then again, she also knew of no motive for him to kill Miss Rosehill. At least not yet.

Harriet's voice was muffled, likely from hairpins stuffed between her lips, when she answered, "Then use the facts. You could have made a determination like that before arriving here. What have you learned since?" She continued to dress Katherine's hair as she spoke, removing one pin at a time to coil her tresses for supper.

"Blast, you're right."

She pulled a lock of Katherine's hair tighter than it needed to be. Katherine cursed, wincing at the sting.

"Language, my lady."

"I could have said something worse," Katherine grumbled under her breath. When it seemed as though her maid meant to argue, she raised her voice. "Very well. I know now that Lord Mowbry was in the garden yesterday evening. He ran from Annie's scream, only to return with the guests. Why would he do that if he weren't up to nefarious purposes? It's possible he might have meant to do harm to Annie, but her shriek frightened him away before he could act on it." What a stroke of luck, in that case, to find an ugly moth with a prodigiously long tongue.

When Harriet remained mute, Katherine continued to speculate. "Mowbry had a personal connection with the first victim. For a man who was set to be married, he isn't making much of an effort to appear as though he's grieving."

Harriet jabbed the last pin into Katherine's hair. "We all grieve in different ways. Bear that in mind. You can turn now. I'd like to see how it looks from the front."

As Katherine pivoted on the stool, she raised an eyebrow. "Does one usually grieve by flirting with every woman to approach within ten feet?"

The other woman rearranged the locks by Katherine's temples then crossed her arms. "When you were ten, you made it your mission to frighten Lady Susanna into fleeing the house. Is that the manner in which one *usually* grieves?"

Katherine winced at the reminder of the horrors she had inflicted upon her stepmother during the first few months. She might have continued terrorizing a woman she now considered a second mother had she not found Susanna crying after a particularly vicious prank. Once she'd learned that her stepmother did not mean to replace or erase her mother in any way,

Katherine gradually learned to trust her. "You've made your point," she mumbled, though she added stubbornly, "You weren't employed with our family at the time."

Harriet grinned. "Perhaps not, but I've heard stories. In any event, Lord Mowbry may be acting flirtatious to cover up the pain inside."

Katherine didn't care to know which stories Harriet might have heard. She returned to the more important topic at hand. "I will admit that Lord Mowbry might be grieving, but that doesn't excuse him as a suspect. His boots fit the measurements. Perhaps he discovered Miss Smythe had another lover. By all accounts she was beautiful, with fair skin and hair. She would have attracted many. If he learned of a liaison, that might make him angry enough to kill even if he does regret it now."

Katherine shut her eyes as Harriet retrieved a box of cosmetics. She held her breath while her maid dusted powder across her nose and cheeks. "Have you measured *all* of the other suspects' boots? What motive do you attribute to Mowbry for the second victim?" Harriet asked.

Katherine didn't answer. She hadn't measured Somerset's or Greaves's boots, and she had no motive for Mowbry to kill Miss Rosehill. She tried to sigh but accidentally inhaled a sniff of powder and spluttered.

Her maid put the bitter powder away, though she made Katherine remain still while she applied a few finishing touches.

"I don't know why you insist upon putting in so much effort for a country house party," Katherine said. "Focus your efforts on Annie. It isn't as though I have anyone here to impress."

"No?" A sly smile tipped up the corners of Harriet's mouth. "I've heard a certain captain seems inclined to keep your company of late."

Katherine grimaced. "Captain Wayland is inclined to glean what information about the murders he can from me so he can solve them himself. He has no romantic aspirations."

If anything, Harriet's smile deepened. "If you insist."

"I do."

"It might do you well to garner a bit of male attention, you know. It does wonders for confidence."

Katherine gave her friend a droll look. "I don't believe I'm lacking in confidence. And in any case, I don't like Wayland or his methods. I don't think he always speaks the truth."

Katherine returned her attention to the mystery at

hand, pondering what motive Mowbry could have had for killing Miss Rosehill. He must have had a reason, though allegedly, he hadn't paid any undue attention to her. Katherine couldn't figure out why he'd found himself out in the garden with her that fateful night.

On the bed, to which she had been confined after trying to steal the cream ribbon now tied beneath Katherine's breasts, Emma whined. She turned her round, mournful brown eyes toward Katherine as she begged for more attention. The wag of her tail betrayed that she didn't feel nearly as pathetic as she looked. Nevertheless, Katherine crossed to her and sat on the mattress while Harriet tidied the room. When Emma rolled onto her back, Katherine rubbed her stomach while she mused aloud. "Papa has never dealt with a murderer who killed two women with such similar appearances. Do you think their physical similarities are of importance in this case?"

Harriet hummed under her breath tunelessly. Upon completing her task, she perched on the stool Katherine had vacated. "I suppose that depends upon what you believe their appearances to signify. You've surmised that the first murder was personal, not random."

Katherine nibbled on her lower lip. "I have, and it

makes little sense to assume the second random in nature, then."

"Then something must connect them. Perhaps you'll need to do more investigating before you determine what."

Although Katherine knew Harriet's advice was sound, she preferred to have a theory from which to work, to either prove or disprove. She remembered something Lyle had told her about a theory he'd come up with for repetition killings, or as he'd called them, "serial killings"? "What if he didn't have enough time with Miss Smythe?" Katherine wondered aloud.

Harriet raised an eyebrow. "Then perhaps he ought not to have killed her."

"No, I meant he didn't have enough time when *killing* Miss Smythe."

"She is quite dead, so I would argue that he had enough time."

Katherine glared. "Will you listen for long enough for me to explain?"

With a motion of her hand, Harriet indicated for her to continue.

"What if Lord Mowbry intended to kill Miss Smythe for whatever slight she did him, but he planned it out to satisfy his vengeance? Who knew they were engaged—it is but a rumor that hasn't been confirmed. Perhaps he started it himself to cast aspersions elsewhere."

She paused, but her maid didn't contradict her. "If he wanted a certain satisfaction out of it, something might have gone amiss in the execution. It didn't satisfy him as it should. Perhaps, for that reason, he sought out Miss Rosehill and repeated the murder, hoping for a more gratifying end. She looks enough like Miss Smythe that in the dim light of a garden he could have made believe they were the same."

For a moment, Harriet pursed her lips. Katherine forgot to stroke Emma and, as a result, had her hand thoroughly washed clean. She scarcely noticed aside from the wet, smooth feel of her pet's tongue.

After a moment, Harriet asked, "Do you believe his urge to be satisfied now?"

"Considering that he was lurking in the garden again, I would say not. I'm no expert on it, though."

"Nor I," Harriet mused. "But Lyle might know better. If you think you can survive without me for one day, I'll depart this evening for London."

"Bless you." Katherine got to her feet and wiped her hand on her skirt. "You can take the carriage. I won't need it. I'm certain I'll be able to manage dressing and tidying up without you tomorrow."

Harriet smirked. "We'll discover if you are, won't

we? Write a letter to your friend while I straighten Annie for the night, and I'll deliver it the moment I reach London."

Katherine set about her task with renewed energy.

———————

"Are you ready to go down?"

Annie beamed, for once seeming delighted at the notion. "I am. Shall we?"

Katherine narrowed her eyes as her detective instincts buzzed like the insects Annie so admired. "What's brought about this change? Earlier, you wanted to shut yourself away for the remainder of the party. Harriet can't have worked magic."

With a broad smile, Annie spread her primrose skirts. "I do look fetching, don't I? Harriet said the color shows off my complexion to my advantage."

Katherine crossed her arms. "You didn't answer me."

Annie stepped forward to tug on Katherine's arm. "I atoned for my past social sins, that's all. Now I'll be able to start anew."

"Your past social sins?" Her stomach transformed

to stone as she spoke the words. "You mean falling into Lord Northbrook today?"

"And spilling tea, and having him escort me to my room last night,"—she pinned Katherine beneath an accusing stare—"even if that was no fault of mine."

Emma nearly squeezed out of the room before Katherine shut the door. Her dog whined and scratched, asking to come with them. But if she came down to dinner, she would steal scraps off everyone's plates. "How, precisely, did you atone?"

The force of Annie's smile nearly set Katherine back a pace. "I gave him the violet-banded elephant moth, of course."

"You did what?"

She must have handed it off to a servant to give to the lord of the house. Oh dear. This might be worse than Katherine had feared.

Annie nodded. "I snuck up to his room while you were getting ready. I left the jar with the moth and a note, apologizing and directing him on the care of the insect."

Katherine pressed a hand to her chest. Was this what it felt like to have palpitations? "You went up to his room?"

"He wasn't there. The men retired to the study for whiskey and cards after lawn bowling. I believe they're still there." She frowned. "Though they should return to their rooms soon to ready themselves for supper."

Katherine might still have time. "Go down to the sitting room without me."

Annie blinked, her eyes round and bewildered. "Why?"

"Men don't appreciate moths, Annie. I'm going to get it back. He cannot know you sent it."

The poor woman looked close to tears, but Katherine didn't have time to soothe her, because Lord Northbrook could return to his chambers at any minute. She squeezed Annie's shoulders. "This will all work out to rights, I promise you." Katherine didn't know how she would keep that promise if Northbrook found the moth.

Her heart trumpeted in her ears as she slipped down the corridor to find the servants' stair. As a guest, she couldn't be seen sneaking up the main staircase into the family's personal living quarters. The rapid beat of her heart made it nearly impossible to hear whether someone approached before she stepped into the staircase.

She was in luck. The narrow wooden stairs, encased on either side by walls without a single nook or sconce for a lamp, remained empty. Gathering her skirts above her ankles, she stepped lightly and paused near the top to listen further. No sound. However, she didn't want Northbrook to happen upon her in his room, so she had to hurry.

The moment she stepped onto the landing, a young woman entered by way of the main stairs. Each froze, startled to find the other. Katherine squared her shoulders and crossed to Miss Young.

What did the debutante think to accomplish up here? Her matchmaker would never approve. Mrs. Fairchild arranged matches based on strict adherence to the unspoken rules of society. The barest whisper of scandal caused her to withdraw her support, or so Katherine had heard. If not up here at her matchmaker's behest, perhaps hoping to trap Lord Northbrook into marriage, it was unclear why Miss Young would venture above.

They met mere steps away from the main staircase. The demure attitude Miss Young had shown thus far was gone. In its place, she glared daggers at being caught.

Katherine raised her chin and folded her hands in front of her, every inch an earl's daughter. "I'm afraid you're lost, Miss Young."

"It looks as though you are, as well."

"*I* am not a well-bred young debutante hoping to make a scandal-free marriage."

The other woman's pale eyebrows knit together in outrage. "Then why *are* you on this floor, Lady Katherine? Do you hope to entice Lady Northbrook into accepting Miss Pickering as her daughter-in-law? I doubt there's an incentive strong enough to sway her. She is very exacting on the sort of lady she accepts into her family, as well she should be."

Katherine didn't have time to play this sort of game. "Leave, Miss Young," she commanded. "If you do, I promise I'll keep this little meeting of ours a secret."

Miss Young narrowed her eyes. "Perhaps you should be begging me to keep your secret. You shouldn't be here, either."

However ambitious, the debutante didn't seem to hold much in the way of intelligence, after all. Katherine raised her eyebrows. "In order to expose my presence, you'd have to reveal yours as well. I assure you, *my* reputation would not be irreparably harmed in the way yours would. My connections run deeper, and the fact of the matter is that I do not aspire to marry anyone at this house party. You do. I will say this only one more time. Leave." Katherine recalled Lord Mowbry, a shadow lurking in the garden. Miss Young was blond and thin, similar to the other Pink-Ribbon Killer's victims.

If Katherine's theory of the killer wanting to repeat his murder of Miss Smythe over and over again was true, Miss Young could be in grave danger. Katherine added, "In fact, you ought to depart this estate altogether. Trust me, it isn't safe for you here."

Miss Young's eyes flickered with fear. Her lips parted, and she took a step back.

Katherine pinched the bridge of her nose. "I'm not —" *threatening you.*

It was too late. Miss Young dashed down the staircase without a care to who saw or heard her. Katherine didn't have time to run after her.

She had only been trying to warn her.

Perhaps this is for the best. After all, if Miss Young was so frightened of her, then she *would* depart the estate. Lord Mowbry—or whoever the killer was—wouldn't have another blond debutante to strangle.

She had no time to stand there worrying about it. Turning on her heel, she searched until she found the room belonging to Lord Northbrook, though she wasn't quite certain it was his, being that it was currently occupied by a different debutante.

Does he invite them all to his chambers?

Miss Burwick, her mouth pursed and her dark hair coming free of its pins to coil over one shoulder, rooted through Northbrook's writing desk. Whatever she hoped to find, it was certainly not the brown-and-purple moth in its jar, because she didn't so much as glance toward that. She sucked in her cheeks as she held one of his letters up to the light of a candle resting on the desk.

It was clear that the remainder of the room—bed, wardrobe, nightstand, trunk, bookshelf—had been submitted to her methodical search, as well. One of the first games Katherine's father had taught her, from the time she was a toddler, was to memorize the layout of a room in a glance and return a single item he set amiss to its original location.

Miss Burwick had clearly never been given the benefit of such training, because Katherine highly doubted that Lord Northbrook was such a complete and utter slob. If he were, his staff would see to tidying up for him. The bed was rumpled, the pillows left in a heap where someone had pulled them off to check beneath them. The drawers to the wardrobe were pulled open, the contents mussed, and some of them strewn on a nearby armchair facing the cold hearth.

When Katherine cleared her throat, Miss Burwick turned a ghostly shade of white. It seemed she'd been too engrossed in her search to listen for another's approach. She whirled, the fallen locks of her hair whipping through the air. As her mouth thinned, it seemed to exaggerate the sharpness of her nose and chin.

The moment she registered that the intruder was Katherine and not the owner of the room, her dark eyebrows lowered over her eyes in hostility.

"Why are you here?" they both asked at once.

The set of Miss Burwick's mouth sank into a deeper frown as the color returned to her cheeks. Katherine drew herself up, thinking to handle the young debutante the same way as she had Miss Young, even if she suspected that Miss Burwick was a great deal more intelligent than the bacon-brained Miss Young.

Footsteps in the corridor cut the interrogation short. Miss Burwick stood paralyzed with fear. Katherine's expression likely mirrored the other woman's, and her heart skipped a beat.

One blink of the eye later, they both leapt into action. Miss Burwick stuffed the correspondence back into Northbrook's desk and lunged to do the same with his unmentionables.

Katherine snatched the note Annie had left and crumpled it in her fist as she searched for a hiding place. Under the bed wouldn't do, because her hips were too wide to fit. The curtains framing the window didn't quite reach the floor, and the wardrobe was much too small to conceal her height. That left only the gaping arch to the dressing room.

Katherine and Miss Burwick charged for that sanctuary at the same time. The debutante squeezed in a second before Katherine, using her bony figure to her advantage. Katherine glared as she crushed herself in next to her. In order to avoid being seen through the empty arch, they both had to squash into the corner.

"Find somewhere else," Miss Burwick snapped, her voice little more than a hiss. "I was here first."

"Hush, or we'll be found!"

Now that Katherine was close to her, she estimated she might be only a year or two older, meaning that the woman was nearing the dreaded spinster age. Perhaps that was why her mother seemed so desperate to marry her off. Katherine would have pitied her, had it not been that Miss Burwick had an agenda of her own.

She ignored the woman's scowl as she strained her ears for the sounds of someone's approach. If Northbrook entered with his valet and hoped to make use of the dressing room...

Well, Mrs. Burwick would have her wish when her daughter was then married to an earl, but what would come of Katherine?

"Lawks!"

Katherine had forgotten about the moth until Northbrook's vehement exclamation. She cringed and held her breath. No shatter of glass hailed that he'd thrown the jar out the window, which would have been her first priority upon finding such a gift. Instead, he started to mutter in Latin, if she wasn't mistaken. English curses seemingly weren't potent enough. From the sounds of things, the moth had sent him running from the room.

As his voice and footsteps faded, she released her breath. Her heart thudded painfully. She shifted to put herself between Miss Burwick and the door. "Now, Miss Burwi—or do you prefer 'Prudence'?"

The light from the main room didn't quite reach far enough to illuminate the shorter woman's face. "Pru." She spoke the word with as little grace as if Katherine had to pull it from her mouth.

"Very well. Pru. I retrieved my reason for venturing here." She held up the note, which the woman had undoubtedly read, given the eagerness with which she had searched through Northbrook's correspondence. "Why, pray tell, are you here?"

"The same reason as you. My mother sent Lord Northbrook an embarrassing... letter."

Although Katherine's shadow obscured the other woman's expression, her instincts clamored for attention. *Lie.* If she'd found the letter, why hadn't she taken it? Why search his desk last? No, she must have been here for a different reason. Katherine's detective instincts stirred to life, demanding that she discover what that reason was.

Pru snapped, "Are you waiting until we're caught here? *I* intend to go down to supper before the gathering notices my absence."

Tarnation! Katherine didn't have time to question her here. Nevertheless, she refused to let the matter lie. She would find a spare moment with Pru Burwick.

As she turned to retrieve the deuced moth from the desk, she found it missing. Lord Northbrook must have taken it, most likely to throw it away.

But no problem, she had the note. The paper crinkled as she clenched her fists. Even if Northbrook was upset over the mysterious gift, so long as Annie didn't volunteer that she had put it there, it shouldn't reflect poorly on her. Although why Katherine cared, she had no idea.

When she'd first accepted the matchmaking job, it was only to get an invite, but she had to admit that Annie had grown on her. She doubted the awkward girl was going to land Northbrook, but she hated to think that the girl's chances at another husband might be ruined because of her odd interest in insects.

She didn't have much time at all to escape the confines of the family quarters. She and Pru parted ways quickly and quietly in the corridor, Pru to descend the main staircase, whereas Katherine chose the servants' stair once more.

It ended in the corner of the guest wing, on the men's side. After peeking down the corridor to make certain that she was alone, Katherine strode with purpose toward the wide staircase in the center of the wing. She passed the chambers of the bachelors in attendance and had nearly entered the span of hallway containing the married couples' rooms when a door clicked open behind her. She turned in time to see a man backing out.

Mr. Greaves.

She'd already passed the end of the bachelor section, and the first room afterwards belonged to Lady Reardon and her husband, but since Lord Reardon couldn't make it... what business could Mr. Greaves have in there?

Katherine fought the beginnings of a blush, for all the good it did her. She tried not to show her discomfort at her flaming cheeks.

She knew why a man would emerge from a married lady's room. To think, only yesterday Lady Reardon had viciously declaimed the Duke of

Somerset for his bedroom activities, when it seemed she engaged in that sort of thing as well. This hypocrisy was precisely the reason Katherine preferred not to associate with polite society.

Greaves turned away from the door and toward the stairway. Apparently, Katherine's presence startled him, because he jumped, nearly knocking over the marble bust of Caesar that stood between them. "Lady Katherine." Greaves steadied the bust.

She dipped her knees as he gave her a shallow bow. "Mr. Greaves."

He cleared his throat. "Err... umm... I was just checking on something," he muttered.

"Indeed." Katherine skirted around him, relieved to see Harriet approach from the staircase with Emma on a leash.

"I thought you'd left," Katherine told her friend as Greaves skulked off down the hall.

"Emma needed one more walk before I do. It turned out to be a lucky thing, wouldn't you say?" Harriet slid her eyes in the direction from which Mr. Greaves had just departed. "Would you like me to escort you downstairs?"

Among other things, Harriet never ceased to worry. She was probably concerned that Greaves might be the killer and strangle her right there on the stairs.

"Thank you, but I'll meet with no danger on the stairs."

Although Harriet didn't look convinced, she didn't argue. With a frown, she warned, "Promise me you'll stay with Annie while I'm away. Or have you forgotten that there is a murderer yet to be apprehended?"

"I haven't forgotten. I'll be careful," Katherine promised.

It was the best she could manage. After all, in order to catch the Pink-Ribbon Killer, she might need to take a risk. For the time being, she assured herself she was safe.

As she and Harriet parted ways, Katherine loosened her hand and nearly dropped the paper she'd forgotten she held. She held it tight and slipped down the stairs. At the bottom, she paused beside a lamp and smoothed the page, curious to read Annie's message.

My dear Lord Northbrook,

I beg you to forgive my clumsiness these past two days. It was not my intention to draw attention to either of us or make a spectacle. Although the transgressions were innocently made, I hope you'll accept this violet-banded moth as a token of my eagerness to be forgiven and forget the matter. It is a very rare specimen, rather like yourself.

As promised, she did indeed leave instructions on the care of the moth, down to which sort of plants it preferred to eat and under what conditions they should be presented to it. She signed it with her full name.

Katherine heaved a sigh as she shook her head. She stuffed the note into her reticule. What madness had led her to believe that serving as a chaperone would be any easier than solving a murder? Clearly, she'd been mistaken.

CHAPTER EIGHT

K atherine slipped into the parlor, the last woman to arrive. Given that the men arrived swiftly on her heels, she believed that her tardiness had been overlooked. At the very least, no one mentioned it, nor did anyone ask about her whereabouts.

However, that didn't stop more than one lady from glaring daggers at her throughout supper. Miss Young must have told her matchmaker about Katherine's interference, for Mrs. Fairchild spent the meal staring at Katherine as though she were an undercooked fish on her plate.

Pru Burwick seethed with ill-contained displeasure. Although she sat two chairs away from Katherine, Lord Somerset seated between them prevented conversation with his overly loud chewing. Thankfully,

Annie drew no disapproving looks. With luck, her confidence would soon improve.

As Katherine ate, contributing to the soft chatter only often enough to keep the shallow conversation moving, she turned her thoughts to the mystery at hand.

Lord Mowbry remained her best suspect, but she needed either to unearth a stronger tie between him and Miss Rosehill, or to place him in the garden on that night. Considering the length of time that had passed since the incident, both tasks proved formidable.

As the servants cleared away the dishes from the last course, Lord Somerset stood and offered Katherine his left arm. She accepted his help to rise, with the others guests milling around them but leaving them alone, at least for the time being.

If she hadn't watched the duke saunter off that night in the garden, she might have considered him a stronger suspect. He could have circled around—she didn't recall seeing him in the swathe of people to attend to Annie after her scream, and that could have been because he was the one that she'd seen running away.

But no. Lord Mowbry's boots fit the measurements. But Katherine pondered why he would he double back to the scene, unless he was very clever and thought his presence would rule him out as a suspect, should Annie have noticed anyone stalking her.

Hadn't Mr. Greaves mentioned something about looking for Lord Mowbry prior to the incident? If he wasn't in the house, then where was he? And his response to Mr. Greaves's question was rather odd—he'd asked if Greaves thought he screamed like a girl. Was that because he was trying to cover up the fact that what Mr. Greaves really meant was that he wasn't inside the house?

"May I escort you to the parlor, Lady Katherine?" Lord Somerset asked.

Farther down the table, Wayland caught her eye, an amused tilt to his lips as he started toward her. Best to accept Somerset's offer or Wayland might find a ruse to install himself by her side. He could nag her until the sun rose, but she refused to provide him with even the smallest of tidbits about the pink-ribbon murders, not when she was so close to solving them herself.

"Thank you, my lord." She laid her hand on Lord Somerset's sleeve and matched his plodding pace. As she did, she searched for her charge. "Don't you mean to join the men for after-dinner port?"

As they reached the door, the old lord leered at the

bare swathe of skin above the neckline of her gown. Although he was an inch or two shorter than she, it wasn't slight enough to put him at an acceptable height to ogle her, if such a height existed. "I'll join you ladies in the sitting room. You make for much better company."

Katherine's cheeks ached from maintaining her polite smile. "I imagine we'll be working on our needlepoint." Not that Katherine had any use for such a frivolous pastime. The day it helped her solve crime, she would apply herself to the hobby wholeheartedly.

"I'm happy to encourage industrious accomplishments. My daughters are all very accomplished embroiderers."

Since arriving at the Northbrook estate, Katherine had seen the duke apply himself so single-mindedly to the pursuit of a woman that she'd forgotten that he'd been married more than once, with daughters older than she to show for it.

Lord Somerset added, "Do you also lay claim to talented fingers, Lady Katherine?"

It could have been a proposition. It must be something in Lord Northbrook's port to make every man at the party so brazen and lewd. She forced an answer through gritted teeth. "I'm afraid the pastime isn't one at which I excel."

"I'm certain your talents lie in other areas."

She would like to lay claim to the talent of ending conversations, but she didn't have that power. Lord Somerset moved slower than a stubborn mule; the parlor, and the remainder of the ladies, seemed a thousand miles away at this plodding pace. "Indeed," she answered, her voice clipped as she tried to think of some way to extract herself from his company. Although she'd hoped to find herself alone with him at some point to interrogate him regarding the past murders and to measure his boots, as of that moment, she reconsidered. She would much prefer to glean information regarding his whereabouts and interest in the victims from others.

"I must admit, Lady Katherine, I am surprised to find you unwed. Is a lady of your stature holding out for a husband of her distinction—a duke, perhaps?"

No, you sarding clodpoll. Somehow, she managed to maintain a serene expression despite the infuriated revulsion rippling beneath her skin. She hated that every man assumed she was good for nothing more than marriage and babies. "I don't intend to marry," she answered in a short tone.

"That would be a shame."

Frankly, if Somerset was the Pink-Ribbon Killer,

she would be surprised that his victims hadn't tried to strangle *him*.

"I would have thought your tastes lay with women more like Miss Smythe, Miss Rosehill, or even Miss Young."

The duke *tsk*ed under his breath as his eyes wandered down her body, lingering on her hips. "A figure like yours, Lady Katherine, is made for marriage and babies. If you change your mind and would like to become a duchess..."

Katherine nearly choked on her tongue. This was her first proposal—and from a duke, no less—only it wasn't quite the happy ending her sisters described, given that he wanted her to be his broodmare. "I doubt I'll change my mind," she said, her voice strained. "I like my independence too well."

And once she apprehended the Pink-Ribbon Killer, she would have everything she needed to remain independent for the rest of her days. No more matchmaking jobs. No more questions about her intentions to marry. She would become a spinster and solve crime like her father.

She glanced down at his boots. She had the string in her reticule but didn't dare feign as though she'd dropped something. With her luck, Lord Somerset would think she'd swooned at delight because of his offer. No, better to leave that for another time.

However, she needed a moment to compose herself before she pursued the true task she'd set for herself at this party. The moment they reached the parlor, she thanked Lord Somerset for his escort and searched for a reason to leave him.

Her eyes fastened on Pru Burwick, who sat next to her mother and accepted the woman's loud criticism of her needlepoint with a distasteful twist of her mouth. Why had she truly been searching Lord Northbrook's chambers? Katherine intended to find out.

When she crossed to stand beside Pru, the young woman jumped. Katherine smiled. "Hello, Miss Burwick, Mrs. Burwick. May I join you?"

"Certainly," Pru said, her voice strained. She stood. "In fact, you can take my place."

"Prudence—"

She ignored her mother's tone of warning and said in a light voice, "Isn't that the Duke of Somerset? Why don't you discuss my horrible needlepoint with him?" She moved toward the wide windows overlooking the lawn.

Mrs. Burwick released an exasperated breath as she watched her daughter's retreat. "Please, forgive her. She's a lovely girl when she's not purposefully being rude." She shook her head. "That deuced Lord Mowbry has her in a snit."

Katherine, poised to pursue Pru, dropped onto the vacant seat on the settee instead. "What do you mean?"

Mrs. Burwick's mouth twisted, and she stabbed viciously at her embroidery hoop with her needle. "She was seated next to him all through supper, but did the blighter say one word to her? No, he was far too busy flirting with the other women near him. She acts aloof, but his abominable behavior hurt her deeply."

Mrs. Burwick had defended him only this afternoon. Katherine wondered whether she could trust a word out of the woman's mouth. For one, Pru had been far too consumed by glaring at Katherine to pay the least bit of attention to her dinner partner.

"She seemed a bit distracted at supper, but are you certain it's due to Mowbry? Perhaps she prefers someone else, like our host." Had Pru told her the truth about her search of Northbrook's chambers?

Mrs. Burwick jabbed at her embroidery again, violently pulling on the thread as she looped it through. "Him? Not likely. His mother has impossible standards. Besides, we're aiming for higher than a mere earl."

This, said to a *mere earl*'s daughter, from a woman whose husband had no title at all.

Pru lied. Either that, which Katherine had suspected all along, or Mrs. Burwick concealed her aim with Lord Northbrook. If she disdained the suit of an earl to such a degree, it seemed unlikely she would send him any sort of embarrassing missive. Pru had another reason to search his room, and Katherine would not rest until she discovered it.

As her gaze travelled to the young woman, who spoke to Lord Somerset with enough frost to betray her distaste for the conversation, Katherine prodded Mrs. Burwick along. "The heir to a marquis is preferable?"

Mrs. Burwick inclined her head. "But of course. He's closer to her age, too."

Than the Earl of Northbrook or the Duke of Somerset? Somerset, certainly, but Katherine guessed both Pru and Northbrook to be of a similar age.

The woman speared her linen once more, simmering with outrage. "This unfortunate incident with his fiancée has clouded his mind, not that she deserves his grief. Miss Smythe had no connections, no fortune, not even a sponsor. I must say, I have no idea why Pru seemed to like her and Miss Rosehill so much. All those two had going for them was their beauty. But Miss Smythe seems to have enchanted

Lord Mowbry so much so that he seeks to fill her void with someone equally as beautiful. Pru's is the perfect shoulder to cry on. He would be very happy with her, if he'd only take the time to look. Instead, he lavishes *Miss Young* with attention." She continued her violent progress with her needlepoint, her mouth and eyes set in a lethal expression.

The vehemence in the woman's expression took her by surprise, and Katherine recoiled. "Perhaps there's time yet," she said weakly. But if Pru had been friends with Miss Smythe, it didn't make sense that she would want Mowbry. Perhaps the friendship hadn't been as it seemed. Was Pru devious enough to feign friendship with Miss Smythe in order to get close to Lord Mowbry?

As the gentlemen ambled through the doorway to join them for the evening's entertainment, Mrs. Burwick set aside her embroidery with a perverse smile. "Yes, perhaps there is."

Katherine frowned as the woman sauntered over to rescue Pru and force her into Lord Mowbry's orbit. Mrs. Burwick did seem determined.

Katherine couldn't help but wonder about Mrs. Burwick's whereabouts during the two murders, and to what lengths the woman would go in order to secure an advantageous match for her daughter. Certainly not murder.

She needed to know more, and for that, she needed to find a private moment alone with Pru, who had secrets of her own. One way or another, Katherine needed to find the answers, and soon.

CHAPTER NINE

S he garnered no answers from Miss Burwick that night. Pru, it seemed, was adept at not only slipping away from Katherine's company, but also at arranging for her to cross paths with people who refused to let her pass without a biting or probing word.

Wayland, unfortunately, was among that number far too many times. By the time Katherine trudged up to her room, she was emotionally wrung out. The one saving grace of the evening was that Annie had been on her best behavior. No one could have found fault in her demeanor, though she'd kept to the edge of the room to avoid being drawn into conversation.

The moment Katherine opened the door to her room, Emma bounded out. Her curly tail thumped the air with vigor. Her tongue peeked out the side of her mouth as she circled Katherine's ankles, begging for attention.

"I suppose you need another walk before bed, do you, girl?"

Emma yipped happily and dashed into the room. She returned seconds later dragging the leash.

Katherine laughed as she kneeled. "I'll take that to mean yes."

After she clipped the leash to Emma's collar, all but hidden beneath her jaunty bow, the pug took a corner of the leash in her mouth and led Katherine through the manor and toward the door to the garden. It seemed she had memorized the path, for in her eagerness she didn't once falter.

Glad to hurry through the chore so she could tuck herself into bed, Katherine followed after her pet without complaint. Feeling a slight tinge of unease at being out in the garden alone at night, she kept close to the house as she let the dog pause to sniff the various shrubberies in the hopes that she would find a proper place to empty her bladder for the evening. The moment the pug watered a well-groomed birch tree, Katherine steered her toward the manor again.

Nearby voices made her pause.

Emma strained against the leash, wagging her tail. She yipped with excitement.

Katherine dove to her knees next to her pet and scooped her into the air. "Shhh," she hissed. "Let's not draw attention to ourselves."

Emma barked again.

"Hush," Katherine whispered. She tilted the dog to scratch her belly. No dog interrupted the bliss of a belly rub by barking. As she crouched, Katherine strained her ears to listen to the conversation. Was the Pink-Ribbon Killer out there now?

"It is a servant. No one walks their own pet," said a man, one whose voice tickled her recognition. *But who is it?*

"Are you certain, my lord?" A young woman, given the demure tone. "If we're seen alone together, we'll have to marry."

Katherine gritted her teeth. That coy voice could only belong to Miss Young. In whom did she hope to sink her claws?

As she continued to rub Emma's belly, Katherine slowly straightened until she could peer above the groomed box shrub and into the vine-covered grotto on the other side. A lantern near the western walkway bathed the occupants in a warm orange glow. Miss Young indeed sat on a bench, opposite the host of the party.

I wonder if Mrs. Fairchild knows you're here

without a chaperone. Katherine wouldn't have cared a whit, but Miss Young's ambitions contributed to Annie's disappointment.

Lord Northbrook clasped his hands on his lap. "I promise to be the image of comportment. I would never harm you, Miss Young."

She laughed prettily. "I know you wouldn't, my lord. I feel safe with you."

Katherine made a face. When she stopped scratching Emma, her dog wriggled. Hurriedly, Katherine resumed the attention, hoping to keep the pug occupied.

"I must admit to some surprise at your request." The young woman leaned forward. "Did you ask me out here simply for the pleasure of my company, or do you have an end in mind?" She turned her face up to his as she swayed even closer.

Katherine bristled. She would have walked away and resigned the unexpectedly brazen Miss Young to her fate, had she not vowed that there wouldn't be another victim.

Katherine thought it unlikely that Lord Northbrook was the Pink-ribbon Killer, but it was better that she remain to keep an eye on Miss Young, just in case. Though, if she started kissing Northbrook, Katherine might reconsider.

To his credit, the young earl didn't take advantage of what was so clearly offered to him. Instead, he reached out to clasp one of Miss Young's hands. "I wanted a moment of your time so I might thank you properly."

For the first time since Katherine had met him, he seemed less stiff. She might even call him earnest. Witnessing the change in his demeanor, her hopes for Annie sank.

"Thank me?" said Miss Young. "For what?"

For what, indeed?

Emma struggled against Katherine's hold. Keeping her attention on the conversation, she absentmindedly set her dog on the ground. She kept a firm hold on the leash while Emma investigated the underside of a bush.

Northbrook said, "My valet saw you leaving the family quarters. I've never received such a thoughtful gift."

Gift? Katherine's fingers slackened around the leash as she leaned closer to the shrubbery to attend the conversation.

"Oh... the gift. Yes, of course."

Miss Young didn't sound the least bit as if she knew to what Northbrook was referring. Katherine, on the other hand, had the sinking suspicion that she knew the gift in question.

In that same halting tone, Miss Young added, "I... didn't know whether it would be favorably received."

Northbrook leaned closer, holding his hand between them. "Miss Young, I heartily assure you that it was. I've put it with the rest of my collection. A violet-banded elephant moth? I've only seen one once, and was rendered too sluggish with awe to capture it."

Katherine sank her teeth into her lower lip to stifle a groan. He *liked* the moth, and if Katherine had only left Annie's note with the jar, then Annie would be the one Northbrook was thanking!

For pity's sake, do the right thing, Miss Young. Northbrook thought he sat with a fellow insect enthusiast, someone who understood his passions.

Instead, he sat with a grasping girl who cared more for his wealth and title than she did his feelings. Miss Young ducked her head in false modesty and mumbled something too low for Katherine to hear.

Northbrook slipped his finger under her chin and raised it. "It was not all too brazen, Miss Young. I'm very glad you made the effort, and I hope to learn much more about you during your stay at my estate."

"That little—"

Emma lunged, yanking the leash from Katherine's

hand. She ran, barking happily, down the gravel walk-way. Katherine swore under her breath as she chased after her pet. Her breath caught in her throat. She didn't dare call Emma's name aloud. Doing so would alert all and sundry of her presence in the garden, where she ought not to have been eavesdropping.

As she turned a corner, she found Emma sitting up, shamelessly begging for attention from a crouched figure in front of her. As the figure unfolded, Katherine's breath caught.

Wayland offered her a lazy smile. "Did you lose something?"

What was he doing in the garden at this hour? Her answering smile was as wan as the slip of moonlight. "She got away from me." Katherine accepted the leash from him. Without thinking, she blurted, "I thought everyone had retired for the evening."

"As did I." His deep voice, laced with amusement, surrounded her like the shadows.

Katherine amended, "Aside from couples sneaking off for a moment's privacy, that is. If you have your heart set on Miss Young, I'm afraid I'll have to dash your hopes."

"You met her during your wandering, did you?"

"With Lord Northbrook."

Wayland clucked his tongue. "Lady Katherine,

you've been remiss. If Miss Young has her hooks so deep in Northbrook, what hope do you have for poor Miss Pickering?"

Katherine made a face. "You know why I'm at this party in truth, and it isn't to orchestrate a match." Though, knowing now what she did about the commonalities between Northbrook and Annie, it seemed a shame to let the opportunity for true happiness pass.

When Emma danced at his feet, Wayland crouched once more to pat her. He seemed to genuinely like the dog, and she him. For a second, Katherine felt her heart thawing toward the man. "Yes, and how are you progressing with your true purpose?"

"I've refused to share my knowledge more than once. What makes you think I've changed my mind?"

"My charming personality?"

Katherine crossed her arms.

"I'll take that to mean no."

She tugged on the leash, but Emma seemed reluctant to part from Wayland. Exasperated, Katherine knelt to retrieve her dog. Her hand brushed Wayland's a moment before she tucked the pug into her side. She rubbed her hand on her skirt to quell the unwanted warm tingle that had started. "You still haven't told me why you're out walking in the gardens so late."

He smirked. "Perhaps I hope to meet with a lover, too."

Katherine stood. "By all means, don't let me keep you."

When she started to turn, he straightened and caught her wrist. The moment he had her attention, he released her. "I have difficulty falling asleep," he said, his voice low. "The night air clears my head. It's peaceful."

She didn't know what to make of his answer. Was he telling the truth, or was he out hunting down a clue he hadn't revealed to her? Perhaps the Pink-Ribbon Killer didn't attend this party at all, and Wayland hoped to use the man as a cover to quench appetites roused by the war.

You're being fanciful. You're chasing ghosts.

She stepped away, Emma in hand. "Good night, Captain Wayland."

As she strolled away, she thought she heard him murmur, "Sweet dreams, Lady Katherine."

CHAPTER TEN

Katherine woke to a cold, wet nose thrust upon her eyelid. The moment she started, Emma thoroughly licked her cheek. There was no hope of falling asleep after that.

Holding her dog at arm's length, Katherine sighed and stared up at the ceiling. A thin, gray light seeped from the window, indicating that morning had arrived far too soon. "I miss Harriet." She would have been able to sleep in a moment longer had her maid been in residence.

With a sigh, Katherine slipped out of bed and set about dressing for the morning. Lacing behind her back proved even more difficult than unlacing them had been the night before.

After much swearing, with her hair hastily pinned

to her head to keep it out of her face, Katherine found herself presentable enough for an early-morning walk for Emma to do her business in the garden. With luck, the guests would remain abed, where Katherine intended to return the moment Emma was sated.

She was not prepared to encounter Mrs. Fairchild quite this early in the day. The matchmaker cornered her as she and Emma concluded their tour of the tree line and returned to the manor.

Mrs. Fairchild, clad in a pristine brown sheath that made her resemble a log, with its high neckline and the severe knot of her auburn hair at her nape, must have noticed Katherine during a tour of the garden. As Katherine stepped past the entrance to the nearest gravel walkway, with Emma in the lead, the older woman planted herself in their path. She wore a dark expression.

"Lady Katherine, a moment of your time?" She bit off the words as though they were poison.

Although Katherine would rather eat her fist than spend time with the vicious other woman, she shortened Emma's leash and inclined her head. "What can I do for you, Mrs. Fairchild?"

The woman drew herself up to her full measure, though she couldn't hope to compete with Katherine's height. Distaste curled her upper lip. "To start, you can desist from threatening my client."

After stumbling upon Miss Young with Lord Northbrook last night, Katherine had hoped that the incident in the family quarters had been forgotten.

"I did not mean to threaten—"

Mrs. Fairchild stepped closer. "Then perhaps *you* should leave for *your* safety."

Katherine pinched the bridge of her nose. "There is a murderer—"

The distasteful woman refused to hear her explanation. "*Enough.* I've heard enough of your fanciful ideas."

Katherine bristled. "Your refusal to see the truth will lead to the death of your client. Are you aware that she sneaks about under your nose?"

Mrs. Fairchild's mouth gaped in affront. Her face reddened. "Do not disparage my client. She is angelic, which is more than I can say for that clumsy excuse of a lady with whom you hope to match the Earl of Northbrook."

Raising her eyebrows, Katherine answered softly, "It seems she didn't tell you the location where I allegedly threatened her. It was upstairs, in the Northbrook family quarters. And last night, after you retired to bed—"

Her mouth twisting in a sneer, the matchmaker stepped back. "Shut your lying mouth. If a whisper of these unfounded accusations reaches the gossips here, I will spread such injurious rumors about you and Miss Pickering that neither of you will ever be accepted into polite society again." Her eyes snapped, daring Katherine to say one word in contradiction.

"You've made your point," she bit off. Even though she would have dearly loved to put the matron in her place, Katherine feared for the potential damage to Annie's reputation. As it was, the shy young woman stood on the fringes of society. As Mrs. Pickering had mentioned, it was Annie's last chance to secure a match.

Mrs. Fairchild, unperturbed by Katherine's glare, smiled smugly. "Then perhaps I'll make one more point before we part ways. If you approach my client again, I will ruin you."

Oh, what Katherine wouldn't give to deliver a comeuppance to the woman. She held herself rigidly, breathing shallowly as Mrs. Fairchild stormed away. *You are above her,* Katherine reminded herself. *And you have more important work to consider.*

Even if Mrs. Fairchild refused to consider that her client was in danger, Katherine had tasked herself with finding the Pink-Ribbon Killer. If Miss Young was so desperate to put herself in harm's way, Katherine didn't have a moment to lose.

At her feet, Emma whined. Katherine smiled down at her. "You must be hungry, are you, darling? Let's find you something to eat in the kitchen."

At the word *hungry*, the pug perked up. Her tail curled high above her behind as she trotted next to Katherine.

Although Katherine hadn't yet visited the kitchens, they weren't hard to find. A small, neat herb garden rested in a patch of dirt near a door. When Katherine lifted the latch, she found the door unlocked and pushed it open to reveal a wide kitchen equipped with an oven, a pantry, a long table for preparing food, and a closed door, which presumably led to a cellar. The door to the corridor was open, and maids fluttered in and out as they fetched tea services and morning biscuits.

After Katherine begged a bowl of chopped meat and a dish of water for Emma's breakfast, she kneeled out of the way behind one of the tables in order for her dog to consume her meal. Two maids entered the room, deep in conversation.

"No," said the first. "I refuse. I will not take him his morning tea. Not after *that*. He revealed himself to me!"

Katherine paused. She adjusted her position, still crouching next to Emma while she wolfed down her meal. Who was the subject of the maids' tittering? She cocked her head to listen better.

The second woman, a bit older, judging by the deep quality of her laugh, said, "He's a duke. They'll do that."

"It's repulsive. Bad enough he pinches any woman's bottom who stands near enough. I understand why those rich ninnies refuse to marry him."

The older woman sighed. "If I weren't married, I'd join him in bed."

"Please. He's old enough to be your father."

"Maybe so, but I hear he's so desperate for a male heir that he'll marry anyone he gets with child. *Anyone.*"

The two women paused at the far end of the table, lingering over the items they were sent to fetch.

"Anyone?" She paused. "Don't be absurd. Dukes only marry maidservants in fairy tales."

"*This* duke has one foot in the grave and fears dying without an heir. Trust me, it might be worthwhile for you to go collect his dishes."

The first woman scoffed. "If he's so desperate, why haven't any of those rich misses encouraged his suit? Half the women here are on the brink of *ruin*." She drew out the word, liberally laced with sarcasm. "Heaven forbid they might have to lift a hand to tend to their own well-being. Except for... what was her name, Miss Smythe? Not a penny to her name, and yet she bagged herself a future marquess, though isn't a duke a better catch?"

Once again, Katherine had to wonder if Lord Somerset had taken personal offense to being turned down, and whether it would make him angry enough to kill. Miss Rosehill had been in the same financial predicament as Miss Smythe, presumably as desperate to marry well.

The older woman laughed. "A duke is a good catch for anyone here. All those empty-headed debutantes throwing themselves at Lord Mowbry and our lord ought to take a long moment to think of their future. Lord Somerset will be dead soon enough, and who would turn their nose up at a duchy? Certainly not me."

The pair collected their trays and moved toward the corridor. Katherine waddled forward along the length of the table to keep from drifting out of earshot of the conversation. Although three other servants remained in the kitchen, they seemed too preoccupied with their tasks to notice Katherine's odd behavior.

"If you ask me, I think he ought to ask Miss Pickering. She always has a smile and a word of thanks anytime I fetch her something or tidy up. She deserves a duke."

Katherine's chest warmed. She didn't think she'd ever heard so great a compliment from anyone.

The older woman scoffed, her voice fading as the pair traversed the hall. "Her? Lawks, if I find one more insect in her room..."

Katherine hesitated as they moved too far away to decipher their words, their voices muffled. If not for Emma, she might have followed. Although their conversation about Lord Somerset seemed to have concluded, thoughts of him jittered through her head, displacing Lord Mowbry as her primary suspect. Mowbry might have had motive to kill one young woman, but Somerset seemed to have enough motive to strangle them both. Judging by his enormous ego, he was just the type to take retribution if they had slighted him.

According to what she'd heard, he had taken a fancy to both women. Then again, he took a fancy to most women. Rumor had it that Mowbry had asked for Miss Smythe's hand. Maybe she had been stringing Somerset along prior to that and dumped him once Mowbry made his intentions known. Maybe her rejection pushed him over the edge.

But that didn't account for Miss Rosehill, unless he had still been bitter over the rejection from Miss Smythe and Miss Rosehill's rejection pushed him to kill again. But Father always said that it was much easier to kill the second time.

CHAPTER ELEVEN

H ow could Katherine possibly hope to test her theories? The evidence from the previous murders was long gone. Not only were they in different locations, each cleaned prior to the investigators arriving, but the bodies had been buried. She had nothing upon which to base her assumptions except the secondhand recollections she gleaned from others. She needed more.

Maybe Papa was right, and she would be unable to solve this case without another murder. She wanted her independence badly, but it wasn't worth an innocent woman's life. The advice Phil had given her at the society meeting ran through her head. *Find some evidence, and use it to force a confession.*

She refused to give up. Her twenty-fifth birthday was only six short days away. She didn't have time to start anew. This mystery had to be the one she solved. Katherine had been called many things in her life, including *stubborn*, which was her crowning jewel. Simply put, failure was not an option.

Throughout the morning, as the other guests broke their fasts, mingled in the parlor, and took a collective tour of the grounds, she relegated herself to a position of observation, paying attention to who acted suspiciously and who could have motive.

Why is Annie lagging behind everyone else? Oh dear. Katherine couldn't see her young charge's eyes, due to the unruly fall of hair behind which the young woman hid, but from her high color and slumped shoulders, she suspected Annie was close to tears. After searching the body language of the dozen or so guests gathered nearby to ensure that no one had noticed Annie's distress, Katherine meandered over to her.

Annie sniffled and turned her head away at Katherine's approach. Katherine laid a hand on the shorter woman's shoulder. "You seem out of sorts this morning. Is there a reason?"

The young woman brushed the back of her hand under her cheeks and gestured to the front of the group. Lord Northbrook strolled in the lead, with Miss

Young on his arm and her matchmaker preening mere steps behind them.

"I know it was wrong of me to hope, but—"

Blast that grasping, petty debutante! She was stealing Annie's happiness. Not to mention that the smug set of Fairchild's shoulders as she waddled along, protecting her perfectly made match, really irritated Katherine. Katherine didn't want the coup of making the match with Northbrook, but she didn't want Fairchild to get it, either.

Had they been closer to the front of the group, Katherine would have been tempted to expose Miss Young for the fraud she was.

Instead, she tightened her hold on Annie's shoulder. "You have every right to hope. In fact, you shouldn't give up now. Lord Northbrook is not yet engaged. He is escorting her in the middle of a throng of people, and that is hardly cause for celebration." Katherine omitted the private moment she'd witnessed between the two the night before. It had been born of a lie. In her opinion, it didn't count. Reaching for the young woman's hand, she added, "Don't despair. The game is not over."

Annie's attention strayed to the woman on Lord Northbrook's arm. "But she's beautiful."

"So are you."

The vehemence in Katherine's voice surprised her as much as it did her charge. However, given the way the young woman lifted her head with widened eyes, it was precisely what she needed to hear. The unshed tears in her eyes made them appear all the greener. "You think?"

"I do."

Annie lifted her shoulders, standing a bit straighter. She brushed a hank of her hair out of her face.

Katherine added, "Do you recall when I asked you to wait until the earl knew you better before you introduced him to your knowledge of insects?"

"Yes." She narrowed her eyes and drew the word out slowly.

"I think he knows you well enough by now, don't you?"

Joy seemed to pour from Annie's every pore at the thought of speaking about insects. How she could be so enthusiastic over the notion, Katherine didn't know, but so long as she didn't have to hold one of the repulsive creatures in her hand again, she wouldn't complain. Her chest warmed to see her charge so happy again. She vowed that, one way or another, she would expose Annie's passion and denounce Miss Young's deceit.

As the gathering paused on the edge of the garden, several women suggested returning indoors to escape the unseasonable nip in the air. The cloud-dappled sky shielded the warm sun, and in the shade, Katherine pulled her shawl tighter around her.

When it looked as though Northbrook would capitulate to the ladies' wishes, she spoke up. "My lord, is there nowhere else to explore outside? It seems a shame to waste a day without rain by spending the time indoors."

Show us your insect collection. Unfortunately, he had never mentioned it to her directly. He had to volunteer information of its existence, or else he might suspect she had been eavesdropping.

The young lord frowned. "I suppose I could show you the conservatory. What say you, ladies? It's on the far side of the manor, but it's quite an impressive display, if you share my interests." He dropped his gaze to Miss Young, a small smile curving his mouth.

"I'm fascinated already. Annie?"

Her smile had slipped. She hid behind her hair again. "I would dearly love to see your conservatory, my lord." Her cheeks turned pink, hiding her freckles.

"As would I," Miss Young said, louder. She cast an adoring expression up at Northbrook. "You already know I share your interests."

Mrs. Fairchild, of course, refused to let her charge out of her sight. Katherine resolved to ignore the glare directed at her. Cheerfully, she engaged in conversation with the group, trying to keep up the appearance of delight despite the way Annie sank further and further into herself. The young woman pressed her lips together and didn't say a word as they traversed the length of the manor to reach the far side.

However, the moment they got close enough to the modest glass-walled edifice to see the inside, which seemed to be draped with some sort of fine netting, Annie's face lit up. "My word, it's magnificent!"

It is? To Katherine, it didn't seem particularly impressive. Whatever material was draped and pinned to the walls, it obscured the interior. Shadows, almost certainly insects', flitted here and there. It looked like something out of one of her nightmares.

Lord Northbrook's shoulders relaxed, and he directed his boyish smile to Annie. "Thank you, Miss Pickering. I admit, it is my pride. Shall we go in?"

"Please," Miss Young said with a sniff. Although she remained on his arm, he hadn't been speaking to her.

He released her so that he could open the door. While the women stepped past him, one by one, Northbrook nodded stiffly to each.

Hoping that Annie would capitalize on the moment, Katherine stepped in after Mrs. Fairchild, leaving her charge with some semblance of privacy with their host. Unfortunately, Annie didn't say a word. Blushing, she dipped a curtsey and hurried inside with wide eyes.

The door opened into a hollow warmer than the outdoors. The air was a bit heavy. The ladies crowded together in a mere five-foot swathe before a netted curtain barred their path into the conservatory proper. The finely woven fabric was tied shut in the center.

Katherine thought it could be dyed in a mottled, chaotic fashion. However, as one of the spots of brown twitched, she realized that she in fact stared at a canopy of butterflies, which clung to the opposite side of the translucent curtain.

Miss Young, on the other hand, didn't appear to realize that the curtain was formed of insects. Exclaiming over its beauty, she reached for one of the bows tying it shut and tugged on the string. Seconds later, she had all the fastenings undone.

Stepping into the conservatory, Lord Northbrook snapped, his voice thick with alarm, "Not yet, Miss Young—"

The moment she shoved the two sides of the curtain wide, the butterflies took to the air. Miss Young screamed and covered her head. Lord Northbrook slammed the door shut. "Don't let them get out!"

Mrs. Fairchild seemed reduced to blind panic as a jonquil-yellow butterfly fluttered down her bodice. Shrieking, she smacked at her chest and jumped around. Katherine leaned against the glass wall and tried not to laugh. At least, until an insect tangled in her hair. *Get out, you overgrown louse!* She waved her hand, trying to stir the air into a breeze that would wrest it clear.

Miss Young bolted for the door with her arms shielding her head. Her matchmaker followed a step behind. As they wrenched open the door to spill into the open air, Northbrook shouted and pulled the door shut again.

The only person in the room who seemed of sound mind was Annie. She pursed her lips as she surveyed the interior and called out for a net. Northbrook blindly pointed to the wall next to Katherine, where four butterfly nets with long handles leaned against the panes.

The moment Annie started scooping butterflies out of the air with her net, twirling it expertly to catch as many as possible in a single sweep without harming them, Northbrook seemed to collect himself enough to do the same. Katherine made a token effort to help, once she'd dislodged the butterfly in her hair.

Every time she caught one, she passed it to Northbrook, who returned it to the enclosure. By the time they seemed to have completed their task, Katherine could still feel insect legs crawling over her scalp. "Do I have any in my hair?"

Northbrook, tall enough that she didn't have to bend for him to look, inspected her and shook his head. "None."

Katherine suspected she would continue to feel echoes of insects for months.

When she turned to Annie, whose cheeks were flushed and whose eyes gleamed with delight, she spotted a thick green butterfly nestled in her hair. "Annie." Katherine raised a hand to her own head in horror.

The young woman must have been addled in the head, for instead of looking off-put at the insect crawling about her, she beamed. Her dimples framed her mouth. "Have I been mistaken for a flower?" Gingerly, she raised her hands to probe at her hair, searching to remove the insect.

"An oak tree is more likely. That's a European oak leaf roller," Northbrook answered, his voice low. He set down the net and approached Annie with his bare hands outstretched, his gloves discarded. "Allow me."

Annie held still, though she muffled a giggle into her palm. "I suppose it was a little far-fetched to compare me to a flower. A sturdy oak tree is far more appropriate."

Gently, Northbrook dipped his fingers beneath the belly of the butterfly, until it latched onto him instead of Annie's hair. As he lifted his hand away, she asked, "Is it intact?"

He lowered the creature for her to see. She examined it, seeming delighted as it readjusted its wings. When she lifted a hand as if she meant to stroke it, Katherine suggested, "Perhaps we ought to let Lord Northbrook put the butterfly away before they all break free again."

Composing herself, Annie took a step back. "Of course." She paused as Northbrook turned, shielding the insect in case it took flight again. After a beat, the young woman added, "But it's not a butterfly, it's a moth. You can tell from the antennae. Butterflies have little clubs at the end of their antennae, whereas moths do not. Theirs are more feathery."

Lord Northbrook nodded with approval as he released the moth to join its mates and tied the enclosure shut once more. He checked the gaps between the ties to ensure none were wider than his liking. "Exactly so, Miss Pickering. I'm impressed. Not many women are able to tell the difference."

"It isn't the only difference. Butterflies rest with their wings shut, whereas moths most often keep their wings open." She bit her lower lip, and her cheeks colored. "But you likely know that. I'm afraid I'm a bit of an enthusiast. I tend to get carried away." With each word, her voice grew smaller. She stared at her toes.

Northbrook gave her a disarming smile. "I have that habit as well. It's refreshing to meet a true enthusiast."

Annie brightened.

The young lord offered his arm. "Would you care to examine my collection, Miss Pickering?"

Initially, Katherine had thought they would be kept in cages or otherwise contained. Was she expected to walk past that curtain into a jungle of insects?

Annie looked as overcome with joy as if the earl had gotten down on one knee to propose. "I would adore the opportunity to look at them more closely!"

And Katherine, her chaperone, would be expected to accompany her. She fought not to grimace.

The door opened, releasing a wash of cooler air as

Northbrook's mother stepped inside. Her mouth twisted as she drew herself up. "What *are* you doing?"

Annie flinched and stepped away as if she'd done something wrong. Fortunately, the dowager wasn't speaking to her.

She chastised her son. "You've scandalized the guests! Come, you must take lunch with us and repair the situation."

His color a bit high, Lord Northbrook shot one last look toward Annie before he escorted his mother out of the conservatory. As he shut the door behind the group, Katherine could have sworn she heard him mutter, "I haven't scandalized *all* the guests."

Then again, Katherine thought, as he resumed his stiff demeanor without once looking at Annie, perhaps it had been a trick of the wind.

CHAPTER TWELVE

A fter an hour spent washing her hair, Katherine still felt insects crawling over her scalp. "Never again," she told Emma, seated on the bed as she wrung out her hair into a towel. "I will make certain the next client I take on has no interest in insects or worms or snakes or any other unsavory creature."

Katherine shuddered. Had she just said *the next client I take on*? No, there would be no more clients.

Although, if she couldn't solve the Pink-Ribbon Murders by her birthday, perhaps she would be reduced to becoming a matchmaker, if she hoped to live independently of her father. There was a sobering thought, indeed.

After drying her hair as best she could, she coiled it onto her head, dressed in a fresh walking gown, and led Emma to the garden. Or rather, Emma led her. As they exited the manor and sidestepped a gravel walk leading into the groomed garden, something hissed. No, someone. Had someone whispered her name? She paused and scanned her surroundings.

There it was again. "Lady Katherine."

She spotted Harriet, crouched behind a round bush at the corner of the garden proper. She was back from London! What good news. Perhaps Lyle had given Harriet some wisdom to impart regarding the murders.

But why was Harriet acting so suspiciously? She could walk up and speak to Katherine if she so desired. Instead, her maid waved a hand vigorously, beckoning Katherine closer.

When Katherine took a step closer, Emma yipped and wagged her tail. Unfortunately, she didn't direct such shameless enthusiasm toward Harriet. Rather, the dog strained at the leash in order to greet a man exiting the manor. A man Katherine would have preferred to avoid.

The moment he spotted his admirer, a smirk pulled at the corners of Wayland's lips. He converged on their position, his posture confident. "Lady Katherine, what a surprise. I thought you and Miss Pickering had retired for the afternoon."

She offered him a thin smile. "As you can see, Emma had different ideas."

A thin sneeze from behind her reminded her that Harriet was near and wanted to speak with her. Wayland frowned as he peered over Katherine's head, but he must not have spotted her maid, for he didn't mention her. Instead, he stepped closer and lowered his voice. "Was the dog at fault for this excursion, or are you hiding something of import?"

She narrowed her eyes. "Fishing for information again, Captain Wayland? You are nothing if not relentless, I must say."

"I'll take that as a compliment. Shall I tell you what I've deduced from your behavior?"

At his feet, Emma stopped begging for attention. She rolled on her back in the grass, twisting herself around the leash. Katherine knelt to untangle her. "Perhaps you would do better to search for your own clues rather than spend so much time trying to guess mine." Giving her pet one last pat on the head, she rose to meet her rival's mischievous gaze.

"Ah, but then I wouldn't have any excuse to find myself in your company."

The involuntary sound she emitted was somewhere between a laugh and a scoff. "Flattery, Wayland? I thought you were better than this."

His gaze caught hers. In the afternoon light, his irises seemed to hold enchanting flecks of gold. "Perhaps you should learn how to accept a compliment."

"When you deliver a proper one, I will."

Wayland opened his mouth, but Emma's barking split the air as she spotted a squirrel. Katherine tightened her hold on the leash. Upon reaching the end of the leash, the pug spun on her front end to face Katherine, flattened her ears, and hunched her shoulders. Her collar popped free and dropped to the ground, along with the ribbon she wore. Yapping wildly, she raced after the offending rodent, leaving Katherine with a useless tether.

As Katherine bunched her skirts to go after her, into the heart of the garden, Harriet burst forth from her concealment. She pointed at the way she'd come, along the outer edge of the box shrubs forming the perimeter of the walks. "My lady, she went that way."

Katherine frowned. "Harriet..."

Her eyes wide, Harriet vehemently pointed in the wrong direction. "That way, my lady. I'm certain of it. The squirrel must be running home to the large oak tree."

Katherine squinted. The tree in question stood at least fifty feet beyond the end of the garden, its branches soaring visibly above the tall box shrubs.

Wayland scowled. "Are you blind? The dog ran this way." He clasped Katherine's elbow and stepped forward, leading her into the walkway.

Harriet latched onto her free arm and dug in her heels, pulling Katherine in the other direction. "No, I'm *certain* Emma ran in this direction. Quickly! You haven't a moment to lose, my lady."

Katherine wrested her arms free from both of them and took a step back. "Will you stop? I'd rather you not split me down the middle in pursuit of one unruly dog."

"He's leading you in the wrong direction, my lady. You must go toward the tree." Harriet's voice and expression were adamant.

Very well, Katherine would venture to the oak tree. However, she doubted she would find Emma there. And given that Harriet didn't tell her the truth straight away, she obviously didn't want Wayland to follow. Why? Had Harriet learned something about his involvement in the pink-ribbon murders?

Katherine turned toward him, hoping to chase him away. "Will you help? I'll go around the side of the hedges in case Emma slips beneath if you'll walk down the middle."

Judging by the way his eyebrows lowered across his eyes, she thought he looked about to argue. With her heart hammering, Katherine offered the one thing certain to make him agree.

"If you find her first, I'll tell you one thing about the murders."

The corners of his mouth tipped up. "Very well, but I'll be the one to decide what that something is. You'll have to answer one question."

Sard it. She had hoped to offer him something small and insignificant. He would likely ask a question for a pivotal piece of information. She prayed she wouldn't know the answer, for if she did, he might roust the murderer from beneath her very nose.

"Very well," she snapped. "Hurry, before she gets away."

As Katherine turned, Wayland caught her hand. He shook it, his expression serious. "We have an agreement, Lady Katherine."

Yes, now go.

As she hurried toward the tree, Harriet stepped up next to her. She hissed to her maid, "See if you can find Emma sooner than he. If he doesn't secure her, I need tell him nothing."

She took a step back. "Yes, but..." Her gaze strayed toward the tree. "Hurry. And don't let anyone see you."

Why? Although Katherine wanted to question her, she hurried after Wayland far too quickly. It seemed Katherine didn't have a moment to spare.

Curious, she hastened to the oak tree. As she crossed past the tall hedges of the garden, she noticed movement along the tree trunk. A figure. Someone awaited her. On her guard, she slowed her steps as she continued into the shade of the tree.

The figure—a man—clawed at the cravat at his throat as he lounged against the gnarled trunk. His copper hair was a mess, falling across his impatient expression. The moment she stepped into earshot, Lyle straightened and turned to her.

She paused. Shouldn't he be in London? She'd asked Harriet to fetch her information, not him! Unless, of course, he'd come to render his assistance and solve the murders with her.

Her eyes widening, Katherine stepped closer. "You cannot be here." He could jeopardize everything she worked toward.

Disgust twisted his mouth as he turned his profile to her. "Of course. I wouldn't want to scandalize your friends. I know this is no place for a Bow Street *Runner.*" Contempt and loathing laced the term.

Katherine's stomach plummeted. She held out her

hands in surrender. "No, I didn't mean that at all. I couldn't give a farthing what these popinjays think of the company I keep. You ought to know that by now."

His mouth set in a wary line, he asked, "Then what did you mean? I travelled here at a moment's notice to offer my assistance in your case."

She fought not to cringe. "Precisely that. If Papa discovers that you're helping, he might render our agreement null and void. The terms were for me to solve a crime on my own."

Lyle frowned. He checked the garden over his shoulder then shifted so he was better concealed by the tree trunk. His form was so lean that, to the casual observer from the manor, it likely seemed as though she stood there on her own.

"I don't understand. If you don't want my help, why did you send Harriet?"

Katherine nibbled on her lower lip. "I'd like your opinion on a theory. If you simply tell me whether or not what I suspect is possible, then I don't think we'll be violating the terms of my wager with Papa."

Exasperated, Lyle ripped the cravat from around his throat and stuffed it into his coat pocket. Katherine tucked away a smile. He must have worn it solely for appearances while sneaking onto Lord Northbrook's grounds—for her sake, not his. And she'd treated him abominably.

She reached out to squeeze his forearm. "I am grateful that you're here to help."

He blew out a breath. "This theory on which you'd like my opinion, it is the one you detailed in your letter?"

"Yes." She nodded. "I've noticed a similarity between the appearances of the two victims. Of an age, blond, slim—by all accounts they even came from a similar status on the fringes of society. It begs the question of the killer's mindset and whether there could be a third victim with similar attributes, or if the first two were killed for specific reasons."

Her friend stared into the near grove of trees. An absent-minded air gathered around him, as if he were miles away—back in London, perhaps. When he spoke, it was with a musing quality to his voice. "Over the past several months, I've studied the history of crimes in London, in an attempt to further familiarize myself with the psychology of murderers and the sort of victims they tend to favor." He glanced at Katherine, seeming to return to the moment briefly. "This all has modern implications, of course. If I can identify the most vulnerable areas, perhaps we can arrange some kind of patrol or other measure to ensure the safety of all London citizens, not only the rich."

"An admirable venture, but what does it have to do with the pink-ribbon murders?"

He ran his fingers through his hair. "I'm afraid that isn't easily answered, given what little we know, but I will attempt to be brief. While studying the records, I've noticed that on rare occasions, some killers seem to favor a certain type of victim. They commit a series of murders, not only ones of opportunity or profit. These serial murderers, as I like to call them for lack of a better term, do choose a certain type of victim each and every time. Some like brunettes, some blondes. Some like wanton women, some the chaste. But there is a pattern of similarity. In short, yes. Your theory is possible."

Triumph soared through Katherine's veins. Her theory was possible. Knowing that brought her one step closer to completing her task. If the killer were only interested in slim blondes, then she might be able to catch him simply by keeping her eye on the one slim blonde at the party, Miss Young.

"However, with only two victims, I can't definitively judge whether or not these murders fit the pattern I found." He paused and scratched his long nose. Without looking at her, he added softly, "I must confess that I'm hoping they do. If so, you don't fit the serial murderer's preferred victim type. I would be much more at ease knowing you weren't in danger from this fiend."

"I'll be careful," Katherine vowed, "but I must solve these murders before he adds another to his roster."

"I know." He straightened, turning to look at her. For once, he seemed grounded in the moment. "While you were gone, I followed up with my friend who investigated the first murder, and I asked around regarding the second, as well."

"Oh?" Katherine checked the garden to ensure that she hadn't been spotted. Wayland, head and shoulders over the top of the hedge, disappeared for a moment as he bent. He seemed well occupied. With luck, Emma was leading him on a merry chase. She returned her attention to her friend. "What news did you hear?"

"By the accounts of my coworkers, who have consulted with your father, it seems as though the second murder was indeed similar enough to the first that it was likely committed by the same hand. Both women were strangled in the garden with a pink ribbon."

Biting the inside of her cheek to stifle a retort,

Katherine nodded. She knew as much already. Had he learned anything *new* that might help her?

"The first murder, that of"—he pulled a small, leather-bound notebook from his pocket and consulted it—"Miss Smythe, was far more violent than the second. The pink ribbon lodged in her throat and had to be peeled away before burial, leaving a visible imprint in her skin even then. The second victim was bruised, to be sure, but that imprint did not exist."

Katherine frowned. "Does that mean that the murderer was angrier with the first victim than the second?"

"If we are dealing with a serial murderer, he might not have been angry at all. Given the records for the few arrested, they seem to delight in the act of killing, planning rather than seizing the moment out of anger."

"If not personal, then what reason can you think?" Was she barking up the wrong tree in looking for a connection or motive? Were the killings simply at the lark of the killer?

"It is possible she was his first victim, and he hadn't yet perfected his art."

It twisted her stomach to think of murder as a form of art, but she pressed her lips together and nodded. "Did you find anything else?"

Frowning, he flipped through his notes until he

found the correct page then offered the book to Katherine. No text was written here, but there was the jagged, triangular-shaped outline of an object.

"There was one piece of evidence at the second crime scene, a chip of ivory. It was largely discounted by investigators, because it could have been on the scene prior to the murder, but I was allowed to see it, and I took the liberty of testing it. There was blood on one side."

Lyle looked quite pleased with himself, but Katherine couldn't see why. If the piece was important, her father would have mentioned it. "The piece might have been there all along and blood dropped on it during the murder."

"Yes, that is what your father thought. However, yesterday I used one of my solutions and was able to determine the blood was underneath, on the part that was resting on the ground. And the piece was not embedded in the dirt, as it would have been had it already been there. There is a high probability it actually was deposited during the struggle."

"Meaning it belonged to the victim?"

"Or to the killer. The chip itself remains in London, but I took an imprint of it in case we had need of one."

"Thank you," Katherine said, nodding as she

handed the page back to her friend. "Do you think it came from a lady's fan? I remember Papa mentioning the ivory as an afterthought, because the fan found on Miss Rosehill's body was intact."

"It might have come from something else. Or it could be another lady's fan. I have not yet invented something that can tell us exactly where a chip of ivory came from."

Katherine squeezed Lyle's arm. This could be just the piece of evidence she needed. "Thank you. You've been invaluable."

His cheeks gained a bit of color, and he tugged on the end of his nose. "Happy to be of service. I took a room at the inn in the village we passed, about twenty minutes' walk away, I'd say. Shall we meet again tomorrow? If you've made any progress, I can render my assistance in providing an opinion of your next theory."

Katherine smiled. "Tomorrow evening? Near ten o'clock, perhaps? The evening entertainments will be in full swing, and I'll be able to slip away by then. I'll need some time in between to gather more information."

Lyle nodded. "I'll be here. But Katherine? Do be careful, even if you aren't this murderer's typical victim."

She squeezed his hand once more. "I'll be here tomorrow evening. I promise."

CHAPTER THIRTEEN

A few short hours after Lyle's departure, Katherine excused herself on a pretense and left Annie playing pantomime with the guests.

After her excursion with the butterflies, Annie seemed in a much-improved mood. With Harriet's help, her hair was tucked safely out of her eyes, and her dimples framed her constant smile.

Throughout supper and the evening entertainment, Katherine had noticed Annie and Lord Northbrook sneak glances at each other. Each time he caught her looking, she blushed vigorously and averted her eyes. Once, Katherine had found him smiling to himself as he turned back to his dinner partner. If the earl's shrewish mother didn't interfere, Katherine might have a chance at matching Annie, after all.

For now, Katherine hoped that Annie would be in

good enough spirits not to agonize over a perceived social blunder. The gathering would keep an eye on her for the few short minutes that Katherine intended to be away.

She had two strong suspects, and tonight, while both Lord Mowbry and the Duke of Somerset were occupied by the festivities, she intended to whittle that number to one.

Motives aside, if either man intended to add a third victim to their list, he would have had to have brought the pink ribbon he intended to use to strangle his victim.

Although Miss Smythe had been wearing her pink ribbon beneath her breasts to accentuate her gown, none of the women had brought such a ribbon to a house party since. The killer had supplied his own ribbon for the second murder, and if he intended to kill in the same fashion here, he would have done so again.

Therefore, if the killer was Lord Mowbry, as Katherine strongly suspected, she would find a pink ribbon in his room. No man could explain that. And that ribbon would be just the evidence she would need to get that confession.

When she reached the guest wing, it was deserted. Not even the echo of a passing servant disturbed the silence. She stepped lightly as she crossed through the part of the hallway that housed the ladies' and married couples' chambers and into the far area where the bachelors' rooms were.

Was that someone behind her?

She spun around only to see the wisp of a skirt at the other end of the hall. One of the guests was going down the stairs late. She hoped she hadn't been spotted as she watched the guest cross the hallway to the main staircase.

Hurry. She turned back to her task. Unfortunately, she did not know which room belonged to Mowbry. She had to guess.

The Duke of Somerset had chambers next to Lady Reardon. The marble bust of Caesar was between their rooms. After counting down the line and accounting for the debutantes, unmarried chaperones, and married couples, she turned to the other doors in the line.

Blast, but she must have miscounted. After all, she'd found Mr. Greaves exiting Lady Reardon's bedchambers, and she was certain it wasn't the room she'd just counted out. Shaking her head, she stepped two doors down to bypass Lord Somerset's room, and opened the door. She held her breath as she did, wondering if the man's valet was inside.

The room was silent and dark, necessitating that

Katherine leave the door open as she entered, to take advantage of the lit corridor. This room was spartan in its upkeep, with not a whisker out of place.

Someone passed by the partially open door, and she shrunk back into the room. Unable to see who it was in the hall, she glanced about the room.

Best to hide in here a bit.

A docket of papers rested on the writing desk. When Katherine held them up, she found them to be notes on the murders. This room must belong to Captain Wayland.

She thumbed through the notes, shamelessly seeking any clues he might have found that pertained to the case. He had copies of notes from the interviews with each of the guests, written after the first murder. Seemingly, she wasn't the only person with connections to Sir John's men.

I'll return later, she vowed. In the dim light, she couldn't read the notes through with the proper care. For now, she searched for ribbon, and Wayland was certain not to have any.

Reluctantly, she exited the room and shut the door. No one lingered in the corridor, so she continued to the next room. As before, she left the door ajar.

This chamber showed far more use. The writing desk, instead of being used for its intended purpose, had been repurposed for the containment of various personal effects. A silver-backed brush rested next to a handheld mirror, both monogrammed with an elaborate *M. Mowbry*. *This* was Mowbry's room. She must have miscounted the rooms before.

Stepping inside, she shut the door as much as she dared without cutting off her source of light. In the dim remainder, she searched the room quietly and carefully.

She found several more monogrammed items: handkerchiefs, cufflinks, a shoehorn. It appeared everything was stamped with his family name.

She found no ribbon, but as she felt beneath the pillows for something hidden, she discovered a hard, rectangular object stuffed in the pillowcase. She retrieved a leather-bound journal, about six inches tall. Frowning, she quickly replaced the pillows as they had been and crossed to the door.

Her heart stilled when she opened the book. On the front page, in a neat, flowing script, was written: *Property of Isobel Smythe.*

Could this be Miss Smythe's diary? Why would Mowbry have it? No lady she knew gave over her diary, even to her betrothed. Perhaps after her death, Mowbry had been so upset he wanted to keep one of her most personal items. Or perhaps Mowbry had a more sinister reason to keep it. Perhaps Mowbry had taken it by force right before he killed her. Either way, Katherine needed to read it. There may be clues inside.

Katherine slipped into the corridor and shut the door carefully behind her. As she started back down the hall, her curiosity got the better of her, and she couldn't help but open the diary. As she began to read, she ambled forward.

"Oof!"

The wind knocked from her lungs as she collided with a tall male form. The diary tumbled from her fingers to splay open, facedown on the floor. As she craned her neck back, fighting the uneasy feeling of being small, Wayland raised his eyebrows.

He clasped her by the upper arms, holding her upright, though she was perfectly capable of standing under her own power. They loitered in front of the door to his chambers, where he must have been headed. *Sard it.* She should have waited until she was safe in her room to open that diary.

"Fancy meeting you here, Lady Katherine. Are you alone?"

She scowled. "Of course I am alone, you bounder."

As he released her, he had the gall to laugh. "Filching Mowbry's boots now, are you?"

She gritted her teeth. "That was not why I entered —" She cut herself off. Why was she arguing with him? "If you'll excuse me..."

His gaze wandered to the diary on the floor. "What is this?" he asked as he crouched.

Darn it! She ducked to retrieve the volume but reached it a second too late. He snatched it out of her reach, turning it over to read the page.

Katherine panicked and said the first thing that popped into her head. "That's my diary. Don't read it."

His eyebrows soared as he unfolded his frame. She stood with him, knowing that he didn't believe her in the slightest. He confirmed as much when he smirked. "You're with child, are you? Congratulations."

She scowled. "It does not say that."

He turned the book and pointed at a line on the right-hand side of the page.

I fear I am enceinte. What will Lord M— say when he learns I coupled with another man? This has all happened so fast. I never expected to fall in love...

Katherine's jaw dropped. "Miss Smythe was in the family way when she died?" And not with Mowbry's child, given the context. She had to read further. However, Wayland stood at her elbow. She snapped the book shut and hugged it to her chest. *Darn it!* She'd given away the fact that she had Miss Smythe's diary!

His eyebrows lowered over his eyes with disapproval. "Don't think you can keep that to yourself. You owe me for rescuing your dog."

Unfortunately, she did. "I owe you the answer to a question," she reminded him. "Not this book. This is my find. It is mine to read."

"You're too set on going this alone. We could be brilliant together, Lady Katherine." His eyes caught and held hers, causing her heart to turn over. "Imagine how much more quickly we would solve this string of murders if only we married our intellect."

She held the diary closer to her chest. "That won't be happening. I don't approve of your methods."

"You don't know enough about my methods to make an informed decision."

She knew that the moment he learned enough to roust the murderer, he would take all the credit and leave her with nothing. When he leaned closer, she might have called his expression earnest, if she hadn't known him better.

"You're basing your assumptions of me on your father's words. Perhaps you ought to take a moment to form an opinion of your own."

She steeled her spine. "My father is an excellent judge of character, I'll have you know. I trust him wholeheartedly."

As she moved to step past him and stash the diary in her room, Pru Burwick appeared at the other end of the hallway. Her gaze raked over Katherine and Wayland, then she scowled and turned toward the stairs, disappearing out of view in a swirl of taffeta skirts.

"Very well," Wayland said, his voice as hard and cold as ice. "Think what you will, but you owe me a question, and I'll have the answer now. Who are your primary suspects in his investigation, and why?"

Sard it! She'd known he would ask something pivotal. Grudgingly, she answered, "Lords Mowbry and Somerset. Mowbry has motive—more than ample motive, after this"—she hefted the journal—"and he was lurking in the garden on Saturday. When Annie screamed, he ran in the opposite direction."

"And you know this from?" Wayland released her and sighed before answering his own question. "His feet."

Katherine nodded, curt. "I found an impression where I saw him run."

"I don't think he's your man."

Katherine crossed her arms, trapping the diary close to her body. "Running in the opposite direction when a woman screams and later feigning concern is the very definition of suspicious, wouldn't you say?"

Wayland's mouth twisted with chagrin. After a moment's pause, he inclined his head grudgingly. "I don't argue it is suspicious, but I don't think he killed Miss Smythe. I saw the two of them in London before the end of the Season. He was smitten with her. Doted on her every word; it doesn't surprise me at all to learn that he proposed. He couldn't have killed her."

"Not even if he learned she was carrying another man's child?"

His mouth thinned as he pressed his lips together. He wanted to contradict her—that much was evident from his expression. However, they both knew this knowledge changed her theory. Learning that one's fiancée was carrying another man's child could move a man to murder. "What possible motive could you have for him to kill Miss Rosehill?"

Katherine stifled a sigh. "I haven't puzzled that out yet."

Wayland crossed his arms. "And Somerset? Do you have a more plausible reason for him to have committed the murders?"

"He's desperate for a wife and heir, isn't he?" she snapped, leaning forward. Despite the stiff set of his jaw, she refused to hear both her suspects denounced in one night. "And he's a duke. I imagine a woman denying his proposal would make him angry enough to kill." She paused as a sudden connection leapt to mind, before she added, "All the more so if the woman in question happened to be carrying his child. If he is the father of Miss Smythe's baby, and she fell in love with Mowbry..." Katherine trailed off, studying Wayland's face. "In his shoes, what would you do?"

His expression stiffened. "I wouldn't be moved to kill, if that's what you're implying." He bit off his words.

Katherine squared her shoulders. "I'm asking if you see the motive in Somerset's fit of rage. Will you admit it's a possibility?"

He hesitated then nodded curtly. "My reports reflect that he was absent from the ballroom at the time of the first murder."

Her breath caught. Could it be Somerset, after all? But after learning of Miss Smythe's pregnancy, she'd been so certain the culprit was Mowbry... "Did he leave before or after the estimated time of the murder?"

"My information is secondhand—no, thirdhand. I cannot be certain," he replied.

"And was Somerset present for the second murder?" She waited with bated breath for the answer.

Wayland scowled. "I don't have access to your father's notes. You tell me."

Although she didn't want to share a single crumb of information, Katherine felt as though she owed him the answer to that question. Reluctantly, she mumbled, "I carried some notes with me. Let me consult them. They're in my room."

Wayland followed her to her chambers, where she insisted he remain in the corridor with the door ajar, for propriety's sake. He gave her a wolfish smile. "Are you worried about being found alone with me, Lady Katherine?"

She glared at him. Unfortunately, both her dog and her maid were currently missing, which she could only deduce to mean that Harriet had taken Emma for a walk. Katherine crossed to her trunk and rummaged through it for the pages she'd brought with her.

When she glanced up, Wayland had approached to stand over her shoulder, craning his neck as he tried to read the notes. She scowled at him. "You aren't very good at following instructions."

He smirked. "There's a reason I became the commanding officer. I wouldn't have lasted long under someone's thumb." He waved to the pages she now held shielded against her bodice. "Well? Did you find mention of Somerset's whereabouts during the second murder?"

Katherine smiled and tucked away the pages and

the diary. When she closed her trunk and straightened, she met Wayland's eager gaze. "It seemed no one could confirm his presence in the ballroom that night."

Wayland blew out a breath and ran his fingers through his hair. "Then he might be the killer, after all."

CHAPTER FOURTEEN

That night, Katherine tossed and turned as she mulled over the facts of the investigation thus far. When the sky lightened and Emma stirred, she took it upon herself to escort her dog out of doors and save Harriet the trouble.

After Emma did her business, Katherine took her to the kitchen for breakfast and fetched a cup of tea for herself while there. She took it into the garden, following one of the gravel walks until she found the grotto where Miss Young had so shamelessly thrown herself at Lord Northbrook. With the way she'd shrieked and bolted from the conservatory, had Northbrook seen past her lies, or did she still have her hooks in him?

As Katherine looped the leash around the leg of the bench so Emma couldn't wander too far away, she vowed to think more on the matter later. Sweet Annie deserved to make her match far more than the scheming Miss Young. Where else would she find a man who shared her passion for insects?

For now, Katherine had other matters to attend to. She had only five days to solve a murder, and she suspected Miss Smythe's diary would prove a vital clue in bringing her killer to justice.

The sun slipped behind a veil of clouds, leaving only a grayish-white daylight by which to read the journal. Katherine settled herself on the carved bench, sipping her tea as she flipped through the pages.

Although she had skimmed them once after the festivities ended last night, she wanted more time to read certain passages in depth. Aside from Lord M—, Miss Smythe hadn't come close to naming any other person. Each of the people in her life was given a nickname, including Lord Mowbry, at first. He had been "Blue-Eyed Lord" or BEL, and Miss Smythe had made several references to how he was *bellisimo*, indeed.

Katherine couldn't help but smile at some of the witticisms Miss Smythe had written. As an all-but-invisible young woman on the fringes of society, she had had unique insight into the *ton*. Had she still been alive, Katherine suspected she and Miss Smythe would get on smashingly. Such a tragedy to have someone so bright torn from the world too soon.

I will apprehend the person responsible. That, Katherine vowed.

Unfortunately, she had too many suspects. Lord Mowbry himself still seemed the most likely, despite the whirlwind romance that unfolded with every fresh page of the diary. The entries ended with Miss Smythe glowing from his proposal, which had occurred somewhat in secret.

Katherine's heart pinched at the last entry, in which Miss Smythe had written of her excitement at making the announcement public, which she would do right after she told Mowbry of the pregnancy. She also planned to arrange to meet the father of her child privately to tell him the news before he heard it elsewhere. She'd been murdered before she could write another entry.

But who was the killer? Had Mowbry been so angered that he'd strangled her? Or was it the father of her child, who had been angry that she was throwing him over for Mowbry, who would then raise the child as his own?

She wondered who the mysterious lover was, too. His nickname—King of Smiles, or KOS—didn't help Katherine to narrow her suspect list. He might be the

Duke of Somerset. Perhaps the word "king" was used to indicate his status as a duke. Or he might no longer be with the party. Several of the initial group, including members of Mowbry's family, had opted not to join the Earl of Northbrook on his estate.

Katherine had too many suspects. Mowbry, Somerset, and even Mrs. Burwick, who had motive, desperation, and a sour enough disposition to resort to killing off her daughter's competition.

Perhaps the two women were killed because they stood in the way of something someone desperately wanted, like a husband for their daughter. She'd be remiss to rule out Mrs. Burwick, or Pru, for that matter. The girl had been acting strangely, and Katherine had an unsettling feeling that Pru had been watching her and perhaps even following her. But if it was Mrs. Burwick—or even Pru—how did that explain the man she'd seen running away in the garden the night Annie screamed?

Perhaps her scream didn't scare the killer away in the way that Katherine had surmised. There was no evidence that the killer had been about to harm Annie, and if Katherine's theory of the killer preferring blondes was true, then Annie wasn't his type, because her hair was brown. It was entirely possible the man had simply run so as not to be discovered in a compromising position.

Katherine's father's advice about never jumping to conclusions came to mind. Just because Miss Smythe had been pregnant and possibly had various lovers didn't mean one of them was the killer. Because if one of them killed her, then why kill Miss Rosehill? Was there a connection? Did Miss Rosehill have the same lovers? There could another reason entirely.

She thought it was entirely possible, especially given what she learned in her conversation with Lyle, that the murders were not personal, and that the killer simply killed for some deep-seated psychological reason. Katherine shuddered at the thought.

Perhaps if she puzzled out who the King of Smiles was, some things might make more sense. Polishing off her lukewarm tea, she set the delicate china cup in its saucer next to her hip. She found the first entry for "KOS" and read through it again, trying to glean what hints she could as to the man's identity.

As a man's shadow fell across the page, Katherine jumped. She hadn't heard anyone approach. As she craned her neck back, her heart galloped. Mr. Greaves flashed her a smile.

"Lady Katherine, what fortunate happenstance

meeting you here this early in the morning. I take it you ventured out here on your own to read?"

Shutting the book, Katherine clasped it against her lap. Seeing as he was Lord Mowbry's closest friend, she couldn't let him see it. Perhaps he would recognize it or, at the very least, judge whose it was from the text about his friend. Surely, he must have known about the engagement.

She smiled, but it felt forced. "Indeed. I needed a moment of privacy." She stressed the last word, hoping to make a point.

Instead, he sat next to her without invitation. His fingers tapped nervously. Was he going to make an excuse for being caught exiting Mrs. Reardon's chambers? He seemed nervous enough, as though something was on his mind.

Turning to her, Mr. Greaves said, "I hope you don't mind if I join you. Safety in numbers, so I hear."

Katherine frowned. Was he flirting with her?

He reached out to the nearest flowering bush, a rosebush thick with white flowers, idly caressed one of the flowers, then jerked his hand back with a hiss when he encountered a thorn.

Served him right.

He thrust his hand into his pocket.

"I'm afraid I don't know what you mean to imply," Katherine said.

"Don't you know it's dangerous these days for a woman to be alone? After what happened at the past two house parties, I'd think you'd take particular care."

If her theory regarding the victims' appearances was right, she was in no jeopardy. Nevertheless, she pointed to her dog. "That is why I brought along this ferocious creature. Emma will protect me."

Upon hearing her name, the pug jerked her coiled tail in quick circles. She rolled on her back with all four paws stuck up in the air, the bow around her neck askew. When she wiggled, she looked as though she begged for Katherine to rub her belly. Katherine gave her a quick pat as she tucked Miss Smythe's diary on her far side, out of her companion's reach.

When Mr. Greaves half-turned toward her on the bench, his air growing serious, Emma rolled onto all fours. She didn't rise, but her tail stopped wagging as she waited for him to notice her.

He did not. "I wouldn't be so certain a small dog like that would be enough to fend off a grown, violent man."

The hairs rose on the back of Katherine's neck. What did he mean to imply? His expression was friendly but nervous. He leaned closer, as if he had something he wanted to say.

"Have you something to say, Mr. Greaves?" Katherine prompted.

Greaves studied her for a moment, then in a low voice, he confessed, "I haven't wanted to malign a peer of the realm, but the night Miss Rosehill was killed, I witnessed the Duke of Somerset threaten her. I don't know what the altercation concerned—and I'm ashamed to admit that by the time I stepped in to her rescue, he had already continued on his way, but given her fate..." He paused, staring at the groomed shrub opposite the bench.

Katherine narrowed her eyes. "What did Somerset say, precisely?"

"Why, he said that he could have strangled her!" Mr. Greaves looked appalled.

Was it an act? Mr. Greaves was the closest friend of Lord Mowbry. Perhaps he fingered Lord Somerset because he knew his friend was at fault.

"Why would Somerset say such a thing?" Although the duke was dreadfully bold when it came to his admiration of women and finding time alone with them, surely he wouldn't debase himself so far as to threaten a woman. There was no excuse for that behavior.

A flash, like an errant tic, of annoyance crossed Mr. Greaves's face. "As I said, I cannot pretend to know what the conversation concerned. I stepped in too late."

Could he be telling the truth about Somerset? Perhaps she had been too hasty in dismissing him. The duke had been notably absent from the first ball, and his whereabouts could not be confirmed during the second ball. If he had indeed threatened Miss Rosehill with bodily harm, it was entirely possible that he was the murderer, after all. Perhaps she should have tried harder to measure his boots.

Mr. Greaves smiled and added, "I only mention it out of concern for your safety, being as you are here alone."

Katherine fingered the edge of Miss Smythe's diary. Had Mr. Greaves known that the woman his dear friend was set on marrying happened to be carrying another man's child?

"Lady Katherine," a woman called in a voice as sharp as the crunching gravel beneath her slippers.

Katherine glanced over her shoulder to meet Pru's shrewd gaze. Why was *she* here?

The thin woman's chin jutted out. Her smile was every bit as bladelike. "Please, forgive my tardiness. I know you meant to meet sooner. *Mr.* Greaves." She dismissed the man summarily with a raise of her chin.

Her tone must have cut him, because he rose with alacrity. "Does it feel a bit chilly to you? Perhaps I'll find my way to a hot pot of tea. If you'll excuse me, ladies." He slipped off the bench without another word and beat a hasty retreat.

Why would he make such a fuss over her presence in the garden alone, only to leave the moment another woman appeared? True, Pru was no dainty debutante, but had Katherine truly been in danger, she would have offered no protection. The tension in the air must have driven him away. Why had she treated him thus —did she know more about Mr. Greaves and his friend Mowbry than she let on?

At any rate, Katherine was glad to be rid of him, because now she had the perfect chance to discover just what, exactly, Pru was up to. She shifted to the side, making room on the bench next to her.

"Pru, please, sit."

To her surprise, the young woman sat. She delicately arranged her skirts so as not to disturb the journal or teacup next to it. Katherine leaned down to pet Emma, who flopped at her feet and wagged her tail, relaxed once more.

"You aren't the type to be sneaking into a man's

room. You must have had good reason to be there," Pru said.

Katherine jumped. She hadn't expected such a direct address. Had she seen Katherine exit Lord Mowbry's chambers?

No. How ludicrous. They'd been confined together in Lord Northbrook's dressing chamber, and that must be the room to which Pru referred. When Katherine returned her attention to the young woman, she countered, "I told you precisely my reason for being there."

"You must have had more motive than to retrieve a note."

Katherine narrowed her eyes. "You mean like you did?"

Pru flinched. She released a sharp breath. Her eyes flitted from spot to spot, as if she was desperately trying to concoct another excuse.

Before she found one, Katherine pressed harder. "You seem apt to wander into odd places."

Pru glared. "The same might be said of you," she quipped, her words clipped. She leaned closer and added, "Why don't we come to an agreement? If you don't mention my presence in Lord Northbrook's chambers, then I'll have no reason to mention your presence in Northbrook's—and other men's—chambers. Do we understand each other?"

Katherine sucked in a breath. Perhaps Pru *had* seen her in Mowbry's room. After all, she had seen her in the hallway with Wayland, but had she been there longer than she let on? The girl certainly was devious. The last thing Katherine needed was Prudence telling everyone she'd been snooping in rooms or inviting Wayland into hers. "We do."

She hadn't wanted to expose Pru's goings-on, only to learn more about what her purpose was. Katherine's investigative instincts screamed that Pru's presence had something to do with the mystery. The young woman didn't seem at all interested in marrying Lord Northbrook, so what was she up to?

With a curt nod, Pru turned away. "Then I'll leave you be. Good day."

Katherine frowned, staring after her as she marched away with her head held high and her arms folded in front of her. *What had that been about?*

As Katherine returned to the task she'd set for herself, to learn the identity of the child's father through Miss Smythe's notes, she found her journal missing. The only thing next to her was an empty teacup on its saucer.

"That sarding cheat!"

Balling her fists, she stared at the empty path where Pru had disappeared. That wily young woman had stolen Miss Smythe's diary from beneath Katherine's very nose. But why?

Did Prudence have something to do with the murders? Maybe it wasn't Mrs. Burwick who wanted the husband badly enough to eliminate the competition. Maybe it was her daughter.

Katherine squeezed her eyes shut. Had there been something in the dairy that would incriminate Pru? Try as she might, she could think of nothing. But Pru hadn't read the diary, so she might not know that.

Then Katherine remembered the new piece of evidence Lyle had uncovered, the ivory chip found at the second crime scene. Could it have belonged to Pru's fan?

If the young woman thought this would be the last they'd see of each other in private, she was wrong. Katherine would not rest until she learned the truth.

Prudence Burwick had to be involved in the murders in some way. Perhaps once Katherine got a look at her fan, she would know for certain.

CHAPTER FIFTEEN

Katherine needed someone's help to sort out the snarl of suspects this investigation revealed at every turn. Thankfully, the day soon drew to a close, and she was able to slip out of the parlor without being noticed.

Everyone seemed much too engrossed with Annie's pantomime performance, wherein she puckered her lips and fluttered her hands like some sort of insect. Knowing her, she wouldn't accept less than the species and genus as a correct answer.

Meanwhile, Katherine hurried to the oak tree, where Lyle had promised to wait. Although the night was dark, with the moon not quite a quarter full yet and often hidden behind clouds, Lyle stood next to a shuttered lantern. A sliver of light illuminated his silhouette as he paced beneath the tree while she drew near. She hesitated outside the golden halo, still drenched in shadow. "Lyle?"

He stopped and turned to face her. "Katherine, at last! I've been thinking."

She met him beneath the oak's outspread branches and offered a slim smile. "You've been wearing the ground thin, is what you've been doing."

The shadows deepened in the grooves around his mouth. "Please tell me you're close to solving the case. It worries me to be meeting you late at night, adjacent to the garden."

"Are you afraid you're pretty enough to turn the murderer's head?"

Lyle blinked at her, for a moment not seeming to comprehend the implication. His scowl deepened as he narrowed his eyes. "My concern is not for myself—it's for you! I come armed. You refuse to see the danger in the situation."

Her mind flashed back to her discomfort that morning with Mr. Greaves. Although it had been daylight and she'd thought herself perfectly safe, for a moment she wondered if perhaps she ought not to sit alone in the garden again. The next time, she might be found by someone with more sinister a motive.

Softly, Katherine assured her friend, "I very much see the danger, but I cannot let it deter me. Besides, I am not young or blond, so I don't fit the pattern *if* the killer is after the same type."

He held her gaze for a moment, silent. When she said nothing more, he asked, "What have you found?"

She sighed. "What I have lost is a better question." She detailed her discovery of Miss Smythe's diary beneath Lord Mowbry's pillow. Given Lyle's reticence toward her presence in the garden, she half-expected a reprimand upon informing him that she had searched a man's room alone. However, her friend took the information in stride, as if such behavior were commonplace. Perhaps, to one of Sir John's men, it was.

As he listened to the information she'd gleaned by thumbing through the pages, he began to pace. He continued to pace for several minutes after she ceased to speak. Katherine fiddled with her reticule as she waited for his mind to return to the present.

He stopped and faced her. "Why would this Miss Burwick steal the diary? Did she know whose it was?"

"If not, she will upon reading it."

"How did she even know you had it?"

"I fear she might have seen me... um... acquire it."

Lyle frowned. "It can't benefit her at all—"

A scream split the air, quickly stifled. Katherine

and Lyle exchanged a glance, Katherine's heart pounding.

"Halt!" Lyle yelled in the direction of the scream, and in unspoken agreement, they bolted for the garden.

Katherine stumbled over her hem but gathered it in her fists and continued.

Gravel crunched ahead.

Someone was fleeing!

She and Lyle pursued them, he a touch faster than she.

She kept on his coattails, hoping he ran in the right direction.

As he raced along, he dug in his pocket to remove his pistol, which he fumbled to load. They didn't have a moment to spare.

They stampeded into the grotto, stray branches and pebbles crackling beneath their feet.

This sodding grotto, with its thick vines obscuring most of the light! Ahead, a figure turned the corner too quickly to identify who it was, down another path and out of sight. Lyle hastened his step, in hot pursuit of the shadow.

When Katherine followed on his heels, she stumbled over something large and warm. As she fell to her knees, the wind knocked out of her,

her hand brushed against skin. Fingers. Warm fingers.

"We have a body!" The words emerged from her ragged throat. She tried again, louder, and added, "Bring a lantern."

Did Lyle hear? She held her breath, half-expecting to hear a gunshot and wondering whether it would come from his pistol or if the murderer carried one as well. Over the bushes, a light bobbed and weaved. She let out a breath and turned to examine the corpse, touching gingerly so as to disturb as little as possible.

No. Not a corpse.

The woman's breathing was shallow, but her chest indeed rose and fell. As the light drew closer, enough filtered through, near enough to illuminate her face.

Miss Young.

Despite the confirmations of her suspicions that this young woman would be next, Katherine's stomach plummeted. She should have stayed with the gathering to keep an eye on her.

The ribbon around Miss Young's neck—pink, Katherine discovered as Lyle neared—was loose around her throat. The murderer had dropped it and his victim rather than tie off the ribbon, which might have been the only thing that kept Miss Young alive. Gingerly, trying not to disturb the evidence, Katherine drew it away from the young woman's skin. She laid it next to her shoulder, to be properly handled later.

Lyle halted at Miss Young's feet. One of her slippers had been flung from her foot. It rested at the base of the bench.

"I'm sorry, Katherine." Lyle's voice was thick with remorse. If they'd solved the matter more quickly...

She blinked away tears. Her voice hushed, she murmured, "She's still alive."

Lyle bent to nestle the lantern against the bench. "She is?"

Katherine nodded. "We were quick enough for that."

A commanding voice, that of the hostess, emanated from the manse. She ordered the ladies to remain inside; the men, she insisted would search the garden in pairs. Katherine had wondered if anyone had heard. It seemed the gathering had, indeed.

To Lyle, she said, "Hurry back to the inn and fetch the forensic supplies you brought with you." With the raise of one eyebrow, she added, "I know you brought something."

A slim smile ghosted over her friend's lips, soon overwhelmed by the gravity of the situation. "You know me well. What will you do?"

"I'll preserve the scene as well I can and search her

body for clues before it's moved. With Northbrook's permission, I'll send for your official help with this, so he won't grow suspicious at your sudden presence. Harriet will be by shortly with the carriage."

He nodded and took a step past her, toward the oak. He paused. "I'll remain close until the others reach you. I don't want you to come to any harm in case the murderer returns to finish what they started."

"Thank you."

He melted away into the shadows.

Katherine raised her voice. "In the grotto! Miss Young has been hurt!" As the shouts echoed around the garden while the men coordinated their locations, she checked to make certain that Miss Young was still breathing. She did, but when Katherine lightly patted on her cheek, she didn't rouse. Katherine stood and shook out her skirts.

Thankfully, Lord Northbrook was among the first to reach her. Captain Wayland followed on his heels, his expression grim as he met Katherine's gaze.

After holding his eyes for a moment, she returned her attention to the host. Stepping squarely between the men and the body, she said, "My lord, may I have a word?"

When Northbrook nodded, Wayland managed to find his way into the path of the other men. Katherine scanned their faces for any signs that they might have been involved. Most looked concerned or horrified—Lord Mowbry looked ashen. Thankfully, no one tried to bully their way into learning more. The one man who tried—the Duke of Somerset—earned a low word from Wayland.

Katherine beckoned Northbrook forward. The two of them stepped to the bench, to a place she hoped would be out of earshot of the others. When he neared her, she kept her voice low.

"Miss Young is still alive."

Relief crossed Northbrook's face. "Thank heavens. I'll send for the physician at once."

She touched him on the arm as he began to turn away. "Someone among us has inflicted this harm. I mean to discover who so this doesn't happen again. Can I count on your cooperation?"

Northbrook frowned. He hesitated a moment as he looked between Katherine and Miss Young, who was still unconscious, then asked, "What would you have me do?"

Katherine straightened her shoulders. "Contain every guest in the parlor and every servant elsewhere. They will need to be questioned, in case they know anything that can help me identify the person responsible. I have a friend with the Bow Street Runners who can be here within the hour if you'll let me send my abigail to fetch him."

The crease between the earl's eyebrows deepened. "A Runner?"

"I know their reputation, but he is good at what he does. And he solves crimes like this one. Can I send for him? We'll need everyone contained for questioning, and so we can search the garden for evidence."

Northbrook released a breath. "I'll give it the evening, but no longer. The guests will be up in arms as it is to be thus confined."

"It will be for their safety, as well."

The tension in his face dissipated somewhat. "I'll carry her up to her room."

"It might be best if you arranged for the guests to remain in the parlor and called for a physician first. I'd like to examine her before we chance moving her. She didn't stir when I tried to rouse her."

The earl looked worried as he stepped back. "I'll send a footman for the physician posthaste."

When he turned to herd the group away from the scene, Wayland balked. "I'll remain to render my assistance in any way I can."

Katherine squared her shoulders. "If you'd like to assist me, Captain, please find my maid. Tell her to take the carriage and fetch Lyle. She'll know where to find him."

For a moment, she thought him likely to refuse. However, Northbrook angled himself between them, barring the taller man from the scene of the crime. Wayland solemnly held Katherine's gaze. After a pause, he said, "Very well. I'll see to it at once."

She released a breath as he turned away. Although she was under no illusion that he would let the scene go unexamined for long, she had the privacy to search it first. And she'd best be quick, in case she found something pivotal to solving the murders.

Leaving Miss Young prone upon the ground and wearing only one shoe seemed cruel. However, if the other slipper held some sort of clue, she couldn't return it to the young woman's foot. She stripped her of the other one instead and laid it near the lantern. Then, after examining the state of Miss Young's stocking-clad ankles, she rearranged the woman's skirt to better cover her.

If Northbrook hadn't agreed to take the guests in hand, the grotto might have been crowded with people who could taint—or worse, eradicate—the evidence. Thankfully, she had some time to examine the walkway and surrounding area before it was disturbed. This was the advantage her father hadn't had. The murderer had struck again, and this time, he must have made a mistake. Katherine set her mind to finding that mistake and exploiting it in her favor.

Due to the recent rain, there was more than one set of boot prints to be found in the area. Carrying the lantern in one hand, she laid out her knotted string in the other. At least one of the prints matched. Another —perhaps Lord Northbrook's or Mr. Greaves's, for both had been in the grotto within the past day—did not match her string. She tucked it back into her reticule and continued her search.

She didn't care for Miss Young's shallow breathing or pallor. Gingerly, Katherine probed her neck, hoping to find nothing broken. Although she was no physician, she believed Miss Young's windpipe and spine to be intact.

The young woman did not stir. Her eyelashes didn't so much as flutter when Katherine waved a vial of smelling salts beneath her nose. She'd always thought that noxious scent could wake the dead. Not Miss Young, however. Could her life be in jeopardy?

Leave that announcement for the physician. Since medicine wasn't her trade, she could only focus on that which she knew, solving crime. She examined Miss Young's dress carefully, without disturbing her, searching for a stray hair or a mark left by her attacker. Unfortunately, she found nothing.

She had barely begun her search when she heard the crunch of boots on gravel. Had Lyle returned so soon? She glanced up.

Wayland stepped into the grotto. Her glare seemed to have no effect on him.

"Shouldn't you be in the parlor with the other guests?"

He paused at the edge of the light. If nothing else, he seemed well aware of the danger of disturbing the scene. He flexed his hands, loose at his sides, as he surveyed the area with a shrewd look. "It seems to me that you might benefit from my assistance."

"You've already offered. I asked—"

"Your maid has already departed. She didn't seem keen to take my instructions until I told her what had happened."

"Imagine that."

Was it her imagination, or did Wayland smirk? Perhaps the light of the lantern played tricks on her. "I'm skilled at what I do, Lady Katherine. Allow me to aid in your search. It'll go quicker."

"I have an aide," she told him matter-of-factly.

"Yes. Lyle, was it? Curious, that you have a friend

so close able to render assistance. One might almost think you planned it that way."

"A happy coincidence."

Wayland took a cautious step forward and crossed his arms. "It'll be some time before your friend arrives. Take advantage of my presence, lest the weather turn inclement."

Although Katherine wanted to deny that any such thing would happen, unfortunately she lived in England. The rain could fall at the drop of a pin. Clenching her teeth, she nodded curtly. "Very well. I'm having trouble with Miss Young's dress. I'm afraid she might be grievously hurt, but until the physician arrives, I'm afraid to move her."

He stepped closer, choosing carefully where he placed his feet. "Allow me. I saw my share of injuries in the war."

Anxious, Katherine stepped back. "Mind the ribbon."

He frowned as he took her place, kneeling next to the young woman. "What do you hope to learn from the ribbon? It looks the same as the others."

Had he somehow managed to examine the other ribbons? Katherine didn't ask, nor did she disclose her secrets. "It is integral to the investigation. Don't touch it."

Wayland shrugged and examined Miss Young's body. He leaned over her to listen to her breath, feathered the tips of his fingers over her neck and the back of her head, and at last squatted on his heels with a sigh. "I don't believe she's broken anything, including her skull, but she may have been devoid of air for too long. There might be no saving her."

"That's not for you to decide," Katherine snapped. "Do you think it's safe to move her? I haven't had the chance to check the back of her dress and head for clues."

"I don't see why not." With a shrug, he gently slipped his arm to cradle Miss Young's head. He positioned his other arm beneath her knees and lifted her in a smooth movement. "Examine her quickly, and I'll lay her on the bench until the physician arrives."

Katherine did as Wayland requested, but she didn't notice anything remarkable, much to her consternation. She and Wayland left Miss Young's body on the bench to search the rest of the grotto once more.

Katherine was glad when the physician finally came. Wayland stepped in, offering to carry Miss Young indoors in order to keep the physician or Lord Northbrook from disturbing the scene.

After a quick word from the host, during which he

assured her that no one had departed the premises, she advised him to station a servant he trusted with Miss Young, lest another ill befall her. Every guest and servant was accounted for and awaiting her questions, but they couldn't be too cautious. She couldn't interview them right away, for she refused to leave before Lyle arrived.

Fortunately, he did so shortly after Northbrook departed. "This feels like a haunted manor," he grumbled under his breath. "Nary a servant in the stables to help unhitch the carriage. Harriet and I managed, with some trouble."

"That's my fault," Katherine said. "I had Lord Northbrook gather everyone in one place to be questioned."

"That will make our jobs easier. Someone might have seen something suspicious."

So she hoped.

Lyle hefted what looked to be a heavy bag. He set it down at the mouth of the grotto. "What have you found?"

"Little of import, aside from the ribbon. Did you bring that new dye you were working on?"

With a twinkle in his eye, Lyle smiled. "I have, and I believe I've perfected it enough to render my assistance in this case. If the murderer left his fingerprint on the fabric, little enough time has passed that the dye should be able to settle into the residue. Shall we give it a go?"

Katherine nodded. She stood back while Lyle removed a small vial of dye from his case. Frowning and with his eyebrows knit together, he sprinkled some of the dye over the length of the ribbon. He held out his hand. "Give the lantern here."

She did as he asked.

As he passed the light over the pink fabric, he mused absentmindedly. "Now, the patterns in the imprint of a finger are complex. There must be a way to isolate the pattern better than studying two samples at length under a magnifying glass, but I admit I haven't yet been able to devise such a way. This might prove useless, after all."

A lump formed in Katherine's throat. "It has to yield something." *For my own conscience, if nothing else.* If Miss Young's tragic altercation didn't help them solve the pink-ribbon murders, then the poor woman would have suffered for nothing.

Her friend pointed at the edge of the ribbon, where a distinct, darker print now formed. "It has. In fact, I might not need to examine samples so closely. Do you see that line?" A small dash interrupted the pattern. A scar, perhaps. "That mark is unique and will make it easier for us to identify the person responsible. Once we have some evidence, we can take fingerprints from the suspects. We'll get him, Katherine."

The breath left her lungs in a rush as she nodded. "Thank you." He couldn't know how much she meant those words. "Would you mind going over the grotto with me, using some of your inventions? It might yield something I've missed."

Nodding, Lyle tucked the ribbon next to his valise. "Of course. But... " He hesitated. "I thought you didn't want my help. You said it would jeopardize this wager you have with your father."

"It will." She swallowed and steeled her spine. "However, a young woman's life is in danger. That is more important than the release of my dowry. If Miss Young wakes, she might be able to identify her attacker —and if so, she is undoubtedly still in danger. We must apprehend the criminal before they strike again."

Lyle nodded, his expression grave. "Then let's not waste another moment. Someone must have seen something that will help us."

CHAPTER SIXTEEN

Hours after speaking to every person in the manor individually, Katherine discovered that no one had seen a single thing. No one had noticed Miss Young ensconce herself with anyone in particular. No one had so much as noticed her leave the parlor.

As interviews went, they were akin to disaster.

Miss Young still had not awoken. After examining her, the physician had not been able to surmise why that might be, since she seemed in fit health, aside from the bruise around her neck.

She breathed normally, and his only suggestion was to leech the trauma of the event from her. Thankfully, Mrs. Young had declined for her daughter to be bled, calling it a ridiculous practice, as if the fright of the attack had somehow poisoned Miss Young's blood.

After providing a poultice made of cooked and ground worms to aid in the healing of her bruise, the physician was sent away. Mrs. Young hoped—as did Katherine— that rest would lead to a full recovery.

In the meantime, Lyle spoke with the servants to glean what he could. As an earl's daughter, Katherine wasn't quite as approachable to the servant class, nor was Lyle as efficient among high society.

Therefore, Katherine was left to interview, one after another after another, the poor sops who had had one glass of wine too many, the mamas desperate to throw their daughters into the path of any rich, eligible man, and the empty-headed young ladies who went along with their plans.

One and all, they had little to say on the matter of Miss Young. In fact, simply trying to confirm their whereabouts at the time of the attack gave her a headache. No one seemed to know where anyone else had been at that time. It was a snarled mess.

Head throbbing, she ended in the wee hours with the Duke of Somerset, who seemed particularly agitated. "Do you think she'll make a full recovery?" he asked.

"I can't say, my lord. The physician has come and gone, so I am certain she was given the best care possible."

"Miss Young doesn't seem as well heeled as she might be. She might be grateful for that expense to be handled elsewhere."

"That doesn't answer my question, my lord. Where were you this evening after you left the parlor?"

Somerset started to raise his right hand to his mouth and flinched. He tucked his arm into his side and coughed into his left fist instead. "There was a card table set up in another sitting room. A bit smoke filled, what with the cheroots, but that's where I've been all night."

Could Somerset be telling the truth? A few of the other guests had mentioned cards, so that part was true, and now she would have to go back and find out who had stayed in the game and who had left.

Her gaze fell to his arm, the one he favored.

Miss Smythe had been viciously attacked during the murder, the most violent yet. Miss Rosehill's had been far less violent, and Miss Young hadn't been killed.

Were the attacks getting less intense? Could the reason be because the culprit had been injured between the first and second murders? Katherine wouldn't know more unless she asked after Lord Somerset's injured arm. If he was the murderer, she didn't want to give away her hand by asking him directly.

Instead, she thanked him for his time and turned to the parlor. Although several of the guests clamored to leave, Lord Northbrook had followed her instructions to the letter and kept everyone in one place. The only person he had excused from this treatment was Mrs. Young. The victim's matchmaker, Mrs. Fairchild, remained in the parlor with everyone else.

Once Katherine was freed once more, she turned to beckon Mrs. Fairchild closer. As Katherine had interviewed the guests, the plump woman had managed to be on the other side of the room, avoiding all questioning. Because Katherine didn't think her capable of killing her own client, she hadn't pressed to interview her. However, she must, for the interest of being thorough and despite her distaste for the woman.

Mrs. Fairchild glowered. As she stepped closer, she didn't bother to lower her voice. "You witch. You threaten my client, and when she is attacked, you have the gall to point the finger elsewhere? Where were *you* at the time of the attack?"

Egad!

The throbbing in her temple renewed with vigor. Katherine bit her tongue to keep from spouting an obscenity aloud. If she hadn't sent Lyle away upon finding the body, she might have had an alibi.

Straightening her spine, she composed herself and answered, "I was in the garden, as you very well know, being as I interrupted the attacker."

"How do we know that you weren't that attacker?"

Confound it! She had never met a woman more blind and stubborn. This entire time, Katherine had been attempting to warn Miss Young and to keep her from this very fate.

As she opened her mouth, Wayland stepped forward. "Lady Katherine was with me, Mrs. Fairchild. We were indeed touring the garden, a ways away when we heard Miss Young's scream."

Katherine bit the inside of her cheek to keep from contradicting him. For what reason would he lie to protect her? As lies went, it wasn't her favorite one. Although it might exempt her from committing the attack, in its place he had started a rumor.

No doubt by the end of the party, the *ton* would think they were having an affair. A more ludicrous suggestion, Katherine could not fathom. Unless, by covering for Katherine, Wayland was trying to create an alibi for himself. No, he was also trying to catch the killer—it didn't make sense that he could be the murderer. Did it?

With a predatory smile, Mrs. Fairchild divided her gaze between Katherine and Wayland. "Why, Captain, dare we hope for a happy announcement?"

Perhaps it was cruel of Katherine, but she couldn't help but feel gratified at the look of alarm on Wayland's face. He darted a glance around the room, as though seeking aid, before he answered in a clipped, harried voice. "She sought out my company for... business."

Katherine fought the urge to cross her arms. Pigs might fly before she sought him out for any reason.

"Business?" The hostess stepped closer, her voice dripping with curiosity and the barest hint of scorn.

Wayland stiffened. "Indeed. She hoped to speak with me regarding—" He caught Katherine's gaze, frowning.

Holding still, she waited for his response. The only commonality they held between them was the Royal Society of Investigative Techniques. Although her aim in attending this party had been exposed once she began to question the guests regarding their whereabouts, she still posed as a matchmaker.

Thief-takers had given those who dabbled in the investigative arts a bad reputation. Would Wayland expose her—and himself—as a detective?

"One of her clients," he finished.

Katherine inclined her head to him by the barest smidge, a surreptitious acknowledgement of their shared profession. Some might suspect, especially those who knew of her father's inclinations and might have hired him in the past. However, without a public acknowledgement, they would avoid the stigma associated with their profession.

For a moment, Katherine wondered if Mrs. Fairchild would accept that answer without pressing for more details. To her surprise, the matron merely sniffed and turned away. Katherine directed her to the corner, where she had set two chairs for the ease of the interrogation.

Although they remained in the same room as the other guests, Katherine had assured a modicum of privacy by moving them out of earshot. When Mrs. Fairchild claimed her seat, so too did Katherine, facing her. The woman opposite wore a sour expression.

After a glance over her shoulder to ensure that the party had not drawn nearer, Katherine reassured the other woman. "I do not believe that you would harm your own client. It would prevent you from making a match and, I presume, acquiring payment."

Mrs. Fairchild nodded, pursing her lips. She didn't otherwise contribute to the conversation.

Katherine continued, "However, I must ask if you

know of anyone who might have wished Miss Young harm. Was there one gentleman in particular who paid her more attention than the others? Did she have a falling out with one of the women?"

"A falling out?" The rival matchmaker scoffed. "You mean like Miss Burwick had with Miss Rosehill? Hardly. Miss Young is loved by all."

Pru had a falling out with one of the victims? Narrowing her eyes, Katherine asked, "Forgive me, to what falling out between Miss Burwick and Miss Rosehill are you referring?"

"Why, they were thick as thieves at the Duke of Somerset's party. However, the following week when Mrs. Burwick played the hostess, the two refused to speak a word to each other. Miss Burwick was particularly cold to Miss Rosehill, who as far as I can tell had done nothing to deserve such treatment. She would have been a good client, had she lived."

Mrs. Fairchild no longer referred to the murder as an unfortunate accident. Perhaps, with the attack on her client, she had grown wise. Katherine sat back in her seat, thinking.

"Have we spoken quite enough?" The older woman's voice dripped with contempt, as if she feared catching a disease should she remain in Katherine's proximity any longer.

Katherine dismissed her with a wave of her hand. "By all means," she answered absently, "though if you recall enough of Miss Young's suitors to guess whom she might have been meeting in the garden, I trust you'll let me know. It might prove pivotal."

As the woman sashayed away without another word, Katherine watched her back. Her gaze slipped from the matchmaker to the Burwicks, standing close together.

Pru looked just as unhappy as her mother. Hadn't Mrs. Burwick said that Pru was friendly with Miss Smythe, too? And if she had been such good friends with Miss Rosehill, what had prompted her change of heart? More importantly, had that change of heart been vicious enough to warrant killing?

Katherine wanted to dismiss the notion of Mrs. or Miss Burwick having committed the string of attacks, but she couldn't. Pru had stolen the diary, and that in itself was suspicious.

Her eyes narrowed as Pru fluttered her fan. She couldn't tell from this distance whether there was a chip missing from one of the delicate ivory ribs.

As Lyle stepped into the room, his back as straight as a pillar, Lady Reardon drew herself up as if she were a duchess. "This is an outrage. A violent criminal is on the loose, and I will not remain here a moment longer to see my daughter become his next victim." The woman clasped her daughter's upper arms so tightly, the young woman cringed.

Katherine expected her friend to shrink away from the woman's glare. Whenever he found himself at her home when a peer called, he froze, refusing to speak a word and remaining little more than a decoration in the room until such a time as he could make his escape. However, she was surprised to see a change in him when confronted by a room full of such peers.

His eyes were hard. He straightened his jacket as he crossed to the middle of the room. In a firm voice with a lethal edge, he snapped, "You will remain at the estate until such a time as I, as the representative of Sir John, have concluded my investigation. I have been granted dispensation from the Crown to arrest anyone whom I believe to be a danger to society. Any attempt to leave this gathering prematurely, I will take as an admission of guilt in this matter and arrest you promptly. I don't care if I take the lot of you back to Bow Street. If this offends you, you can take it up with Sir John at your hearing."

The air rippled in the wake of his words. Several lords and ladies bristled, but their expressions held enough shadows of fear that they didn't contradict him. In the silence, her friend turned to her, his expression every bit as sharp and authoritative.

"Lady Katherine, a word?"

She inclined her head. "Of course, Mr. Murphy. I'm done here."

As he turned, he said, "Then you are all free to return to your rooms if it pleases you. Lady Katherine and I will discuss tonight's proceedings."

Katherine's head throbbed as the guests hesitantly filed past. Her eyes were glued on Pru's fan, but she didn't see any chips missing from the ivory. Perhaps she had another fan.

When Lord Northbrook stepped near at the tail of the procession, he stopped to clasp Lyle's forearm and whisper, "Godspeed."

Godspeed, indeed. If Lyle hadn't gleaned anything more useful than Katherine, they would be in for a long and thorny journey to apprehend the murderer.

CHAPTER SEVENTEEN

The servants had seen no more than the guests, though to their credit it had been because most were abed and the others awaited their masters' return. However, none of their interviews aided with their search for the Pink-Ribbon Killer. They exchanged information in the parlor until Katherine could barely keep her eyes open. Only then did Lyle urge her to get some rest. He had been given lodging in the manor for the night.

Even after she parted from him, her mind drowned in the details of the murders. Emma snored fitfully, woofing from time to time and kicking her feet. Katherine couldn't seem to close her eyes without seeing Miss Young's pale-as-death face and the ribbon around her neck.

If Katherine had only solved the mystery sooner,

she might have been able to prevent Miss Young from coming to any harm. If she'd paid more attention to Miss Young's whereabouts before she'd left... From the very start, she'd suspected there would be another victim. Perhaps, deep down, she had hoped that an attack of this nature would occur. Now they had the imprint on the ribbon that the killer had left behind. Unfortunately, it was all the evidence they had. That, and her suspicions.

Restless, Katherine rose and dressed in a simple frock, leaving her laces loose. She donned her dressing gown and scooped Emma off the bed. Perhaps the dog would enjoy a midnight jaunt to the kitchen.

Instead of her usual enthusiasm, the pug tucked her face into Katherine's side and fell asleep once more. If not for the murderer on the loose, Katherine might have left her in bed to sleep, but she wanted some form of protection tonight. For all her miniscule size, Katherine knew that if Emma were ever riled, she would defend Katherine with her life.

So armed, Katherine left her room in search of some warm milk in the kitchen. She took the main staircase to the first level and tiptoed down the corridor with a candle in one hand and Emma in the other.

Ahead, more candlelight flickered in patterns over the open library door. Who was awake at this hour?

Cautiously, Katherine slowed her step as she neared. Her dog didn't stir.

When she reached the door to the library and peeked inside, she found the room still and silent. Shelves of books framed the walls on all sides. In the center, a wingback chair faced the unlit hearth on the far end of the room. Two other chairs flanked it, with a small table in between. On one such table, a candle guttered. On another, a decanter of amber liquid rested next to an empty tumbler with a few sips still left in the bottom.

What simpleton had fallen so deep in his cups that he forgot the candle alight? He could burn the house down! Releasing an exasperated breath, she crossed to blow it out before it toppled and set the manor ablaze.

Before she reached midway, a man's hand shot out to the side to grip the decanter. He popped open the top, splashed whiskey into his glass, then returned the decanter to its place.

Taken unawares, Katherine jumped. Her hold tightened briefly on Emma, who yelped awake. The man in the chair whirled, sloshing liquid onto the leather arm.

"Who's there?" Lord Mowbry's voice slurred. Upon seeing her, he grimaced and turned around again. "Leave me be, my lady."

She might have turned on her heel, had Emma not started to squirm. Katherine approached the chairs to set the candle next to the stump of his while she adjusted her hold on her dog. "Hush now, Emma."

When she caught a glimpse of Mowbry's face, she saw such bald pain there that she couldn't turn and obey his edict. He looked liable to drink himself to death if she did. Instead, she set her dog on the chair and gathered the decanter and tumbler to keep it out of his reach.

Mowbry moved as if to stand, but Emma lurched off the chair and bounded to him. When she rose up on her hind legs, she planted her front paws on his knee. He sighed and patted the dog as he resignedly remarked, "Don't you know not to keep a man from his drink, Lady Katherine?"

She placed the decanter and tumbler on the mantel over the cold hearth before she turned. "I'm surprised your friend Mr. Greaves isn't here doing precisely this."

The young lord stared into his hands until Emma nudged him with her nose. He wearily rubbed her head. "This latest attack. It reminds me of—" His voice cracked. "Of..."

Miss Smythe. "I know." Katherine's words fell heavy into the silence.

Mowbry still didn't look at her. His expression was heavy, lines of agony curling around his mouth and nose.

"You loved her very much, didn't you?"

Running his fingers along the curve of Emma's ear, Mowbry collected his thoughts. After a moment, he sighed. "Of course I did. I asked her to marry me."

Given that Mowbry had been in possession of her diary, he likely knew that she had been in the family way. Katherine took a gamble. "I wager you did so even after knowing of her state."

Mowbry jerked his head up to look at her, distaste clear across his face. "So you're the thief."

"I'll have her diary back in your hands as soon as may be."

When he clenched his fist on his knee, Emma shrank back onto the floor. She crawled back to Katherine, who patted her to reassure her.

His voice thick with outrage and barely decipherable due to his slurred speech, Mowbry said, "You have no right to look at that. It's private."

"It might help to identify her murderer. Unless you happen to know the father?"

Mowbry flinched. He careened back into the chair. If it had been any less sturdy, it might have fallen backward with him in it. "I don't know," he admitted softly.

Tarnation. That would have helped. "What do you know?" Katherine asked.

He returned to staring at his hands. "She told me, of her... state. I told her it didn't sodding matter. I didn't care if she gave birth to a son and he became my heir. All I wanted in my life was Isobel." He grew silent. After a moment, just as Katherine was tempted to prompt him further, he added, "I know, that night, she was going to see him. To tell him that she was to become my bride and end their liaison. Do you think..." His voice broke, and he raised his gaze. "Do you think he killed her? The father of her child? In doing so, he would have killed his own child." His voice was vehement, thick with disbelief, as though he couldn't fathom such an atrocity.

And yet it might very well have happened.

"It's possible," Katherine said softly. "No matter who committed this crime, I will see him brought to justice. I will see him hanged."

A man cleared his throat behind them. When Emma stiffened, clearly as startled over the new arrival as Katherine, she turned to see Mr. Greaves.

"Mowbry, old chap, are you feeling quite the

thing?" He held Katherine's gaze a moment more before turning his gaze to his friend.

Leaning over, Katherine scooped Emma into her arms before standing and collecting her candle. "Forgive me, gentlemen. I don't mean to intrude. Good night."

Katherine hurried into the hall then slowed her pace, her thoughts centered on Mowbry's obviously distraught state. It didn't seem likely that he had killed Miss Smythe, unless his state was borne of guilt more than grief. The men's voices drifted out into the hall as she made her way back to her room.

"I knocked on your door. You didn't answer. Should I be worried?" Mr. Greaves, his voice still hard, didn't sound the least bit worried.

Lord Mowbry didn't appear to notice. Sullen, he asked, "Are you here to check up on me, Monty?"

"My family hasn't held a title in generations. I'm no more a Montrose than you are a king. I wanted to borrow your bloody riding boots to go out in the morning. I didn't bring any, and Lady..."

Katherine slipped down the corridor and out of earshot. When she reached the second floor, she set Emma on the ground and opened her door. The moment she was inside, she shut and locked it.

Even if she had gleaned new information

regarding the investigation tonight, she shouldn't have been out of bed. The Pink-Ribbon Killer had failed with Miss Young. And now he likely knew Katherine was trying to figure out his identity.

The manor wasn't safe for anyone until he was caught.

CHAPTER EIGHTEEN

K atherine must have mulled over the facts in her sleep, because when she woke, her next move was fresh in her mind. She either needed additional evidence to warrant looking at the suspects' fingers to match them to the ribbon, or she needed to talk to Miss Young. She hoped that Miss Young had awakened during the night.

Due to her late night, she woke up late. After dressing and begging Harriet to look after Annie and Emma, Katherine slipped into the corridor. Straggling guests greeted each other sleepily as they descended for breakfast. Katherine waited until she was the last in the hall before she found Miss Young's room. She rapped on the door.

Mrs. Young, a more mature model of her daughter, opened the door. Her blond hair, graying at the temples, fell in disarray around her shoulders. Her eyes were bloodshot. She looked as though she hadn't gotten a wink of sleep.

Gently, Katherine smiled at her, encouraging her. Did she, like Mrs. Fairchild, suspect Katherine of harming her daughter? "Good morning, Mrs. Young. I came to inquire after your daughter. Has she seen any improvement?"

The older woman's face crumpled, and she hugged herself. Tears gathered in the corners of her eyes as she shook her head. "She is the same as last night. Perhaps I was wrong to send the physician away without bleeding her..."

Katherine laid her hand over the other woman's. "You did nothing wrong. This is an impossible situation. I am so terribly sorry that you were put in this position."

"Mrs. Fairchild tells me you knew of the attack. You warned my daughter to leave?"

She nodded. "I did." If only Miss Young had taken heed.

Caution rippled across Mrs. Young's face. "How did you know? Do you know who did this?" Her voice sharpened with every word.

"If I did, he would already be on his way to Newgate, I assure you, Mrs. Young. I had my suspicions, is all. Your daughter greatly resembles the other two victims."

The older woman clasped her hand to her chest. "You think there's some monster going out and killing off young blond women?"

"Yes. I do."

"You think he's in this *house*?"

"I do, but—"

Mrs. Young took a step back as though struck. Katherine blocked the doorway, lest the other woman decide to shut her out.

"Mrs. Young, please, I implore you. The moment your daughter awakens, I must speak with her. We must find the person responsible."

"*You.*"

Katherine jumped at the new, venom-laced voice. She turned as Mrs. Fairchild squeezed past her into the room. The matchmaker wagged her finger in Katherine's face.

"Be gone, pest. It is *your* fault Miss Young is in this situation. You... you drew attention to her or... encouraged her disobedience!"

Seemingly, Katherine would learn no further information from Mrs. Young, not while the matchmaker remained within earshot. Katherine stiffly bid them both adieu and turned as they shut the door.

Without Miss Young's experiences last night, Katherine would make no further progress as to the identity of the killer, at least not without finding further evidence. Again, Miss Young's pallid face flashed in front of her eyes, the ribbon twined around her neck. Where had the attacker found that ribbon?

He—or she—must have brought it to the manor. Katherine hadn't found any ribbon in Lord Mowbry's room, and after seeing how distraught he was last night, she couldn't in earnestness believe he was the villain, unless his distress was not about how the attack reminded him of Miss Smythe but instead about regret for not being able to finish the job with Miss Young.

The pink ribbon was the key. Did the killer have a supply of them? Katherine meant to find out.

However, she couldn't predict when those below would return after breakfast. She needed an excuse for finding herself in someone's chamber. She needed a dog more apt to misbehave than saunter neatly down the stairs.

Fortunately, when she peeked into her room once more, she found just such a volunteer. Harriet wasn't within and must have been partaking in breakfast or attending to some other chore. Emma bounced around Katherine's legs as she called the dog closer.

"Stay with me, girl," she whispered as she beckoned the dog into the corridor. Emma seemed happy enough to do as she was told.

Katherine began by searching the gentlemen's rooms. Wayland, unfortunately, had moved his notes to a different location. As she gave his rooms a cursory search, Emma trotted up and dropped a hairbrush at her feet. It was not Wayland's hairbrush.

That little thief! Katherine groaned under her breath. To which room did the brush belong? She snatched it and entered the hall, meaning to return it once she peeked into a few doors and discovered which chamber lacked a hairbrush. It took her but moments.

When she turned, Emma deposited a glove at her toe. That was followed by a handkerchief, a pocket watch, a slim volume of frighteningly erotic poetry, and a belt. Each time, Katherine hurried from door to door to discover the correct owner and return the items. She tried to keep an eye on Emma whilst she was inside to prevent her dog from pilfering anything else, but it proved impossible.

By the time she entered the hall again, Emma had found yet another item, and her time to search the rooms drew shorter by the minute. When Emma brought her a man's set of drawers, she stuffed them in the nearest vase. Katherine did not care to examine them closely enough to determine their owner. How did Emma manage? She had to have a pile of items stashed somewhere along the corridor, but Katherine didn't have time to search for it now. She had to find those ribbons.

And find them, indeed she did—in the most surprising place.

Mrs. Burwick's chambers.

Would she be foolhardy enough to bring such an infamous color for her daughter? Or was she the murderer? Katherine's head throbbed as she shut her eyes and tried to recall if the figure she had seen in the garden yesterday evening might have been a woman.

Had the silhouette been tall, short? Confound it, but she couldn't remember. Lyle had been in front of her, bolting after the culprit when Katherine had tripped over the body. Miss Young's face, she could recall in excruciating detail, but every other detail of the encounter was a blur. She would have to ask Lyle. For now, she stuffed the ribbon into her reticule.

The fan! Katherine made haste to rummage through drawers and in the armoire, but no fan could be found.

When she returned to the corridor, Emma dropped her rump to the ground and deposited a snuffbox at Katherine's feet.

Sarding dog! She breathed deeply through her nose so she didn't snap at her beloved pet. Once she had herself under control, she made certain the doors along the corridor were all shut. Where was that dog hiding the items she stole? Katherine sighed and snatched up the snuffbox.

It looked more like an heirloom than a box in use, the ivory lid pockmarked with chips that nearly obscured the monogrammed *M*. At least that was easy to place—only one Lord M in her acquaintance enjoyed monogramming everything he owned. As soon as she replaced the snuffbox in Mowbry's chambers, she would shut Emma away and find her stash.

Katherine laid her hand on the latch, when a man stepped up the stairs and into the corridor, where she was in plain view.

Darn it! She'd been caught.

CHAPTER NINETEEN

Katherine stuffed the snuffbox behind her back as she turned to face Captain Wayland. What was he doing here? He had an unfortunate habit of manifesting precisely when she didn't want his presence. Not, come to think of it, that she ever craved the sight of him.

He stopped just out of arm's reach and raised his eyebrows. "You look conspicuous."

"As do you. Everyone is down at breakfast. Why are you not with them?"

His brows raised by another notch. "I finished eating."

Had he? Or had he simply noticed her absence and sought her out? She scowled. "You're following me."

"Do I have a right to wonder at your activities?

What do you have behind your back?" He craned his neck, but Katherine shifted to hide the snuffbox. Thank heavens for her height!

"What business do you have here?" He gestured behind her. "Here, being the door to my room?"

Damnation! She'd forgotten for a moment that his room was next to Lord Mowbry's.

"Have you robbed me?" he asked. One corner of his mouth curled up as though he was amused.

"I have not." Sadly, Katherine couldn't speak for Emma. She still hadn't found that wily dog's stash.

The pug butted against Wayland's leg, shamelessly begging for attention. For the moment, he ignored her in favor of scrutinizing Katherine.

Could he be following her to make certain she didn't find the murderer?

It seemed ludicrous to suspect him, but she now realized that everyone had readily believed the lie that he had been with her at the time of the attack, which meant he hadn't been in the parlor with the other guests. Was that why he'd lied for her? By providing Katherine with an alibi, he had also excused himself from suspicion. But he couldn't be the murderer, for he hadn't been a guest at the other house parties!

Or had he? A man of Wayland's reputation might have been able to slip away or bribe his way out of the report given by Sir John's men. Perhaps Papa had left his name off the list because he didn't want to consider a fellow detective, even one whose methods he despised, as a suspect. If there was even the slightest possibility that Wayland might have been present for the other two attacks...

Her suspicions must have shown on her face, because he grimaced. "Please tell me you don't suspect *I* am in league with the murderer. For the love of Jove, I've been begging you to join forces since the moment you arrived. I want to apprehend the killer every bit as much as you do."

Katherine adjusted her hands behind her. The worn snuffbox was irrelevant, but if Wayland found the ribbons in her reticule, he would know that her main suspects had changed. In an effort to keep one step ahead of him—at the very least, until she discovered whether or not he was involved—she said, "You're right. There is a murderer on the loose. We should share information."

He narrowed his eyes. "Why the sudden change of heart?"

"The murderer is still at large. He might try again with Miss Young. A woman's life hangs in the balance." Guilt stung her chest as she spoke the words, for they were true. Was she being unduly stubborn in not sharing her every suspicion with Wayland? She didn't want him to take credit for catching the murderer, but telling him might expedite their search, and as she'd told Lyle, this concerned something far more important than money.

For the moment, she held her tongue on the matter.

Fortunately, Wayland seemed to accept her answer. "Did you and your friend find anything at the crime scene?"

"Nothing conclusive," she admitted. At least she could speak the truth about that. "Have you noticed the way Somerset favors his right arm?"

Wayland pressed his lips together as he thought. "I have. Do you think that excuses him as a suspect?"

"To the contrary," she said hurriedly. "The violence of the crimes seems to have decreased drastically since the first. If his arm was injured in between the first and second murders, that might account for the discrepancy."

"Or they were committed by two separate people," he countered.

Katherine's heart skipped a beat. *Please, tell me I am not searching for two separate criminals.*

Mrs. Burwick had a motive for every murder—the girls were prettier than Pru, perhaps in line to marry wealthy men that she hoped to connect herself with through her daughter. Not to mention, she had the ribbon. Then again, Pru shared the room with her mother. Perhaps the ribbons belonged to Pru.

She asked Wayland, "Do you know when Somerset injured his arm?" Her voice was a bit waspish, and she forced herself to soften her tone. "The information is pivotal to my theory." *To my secondary theory, at the moment.*

"He injured it after his house party."

Perhaps her secondary theory had more merit than she thought. "Are you certain?"

"I was there. He injured it during a phaeton race through London, competing with some of the young bucks. I believe Miss Rosehill was there at the time, and they were vying for her attention."

Another tie to the murders. "Miss Rosehill? Not Miss Burwick, as well?" If they had been friends, something might have happened at that phaeton race to cause a rift between them.

"No. Her aunt—a widow, I believe—and a... friend of another racer, was her only company that night."

So Miss Rosehill and Pru had already had a falling out by that point. The reason remained a mystery Katherine wanted to investigate, but she had no more time alone with Wayland. As footsteps echoed up the stairs, Katherine quickly bid him adieu and gathered Emma. She turned away, clenching the snuffbox so hard it dug into her palm.

Could Lord Somerset's injury be the reason for the decreased violence between the first and second murders? If not for the ribbons in her reticule, Katherine might have been inclined to think him the best suspect in the matter.

She didn't know for certain. But soon she would.

CHAPTER TWENTY

Mrs. Burwick hadn't been among those to go out on a ride come the morning, because she was especially deft at evading detection when she didn't want to be found.

Once Katherine located Lyle, she informed him of her discovery, and they agreed to confront Mrs. Burwick on the matter and hear what she had to say. After all, as Lyle pointed out, they were only ribbons. They held no traces of blood or anything nefarious, although they matched the ribbon found around Miss Young's neck in both fabric and color.

"Are you certain you wouldn't like to wear one in your hair?" Katherine teased. With everyone else resting from their morning ride or else occupied somewhere in the manor, they had the guest-wing corridor to themselves. The prolonged wait grated on her nerves. Where was Mrs. Burwick, and what mischief did she enact at that moment?

Ceasing his constant shifting from foot to foot, Lyle leaned against the wall outside the door to Mrs. Burwick's chamber and countered, "I think the color suits you better."

Katherine laughed, more a nervous sound than one of mirth. "Imagine the looks on everyone's faces if I came down to supper with a pink ribbon in my hair. Perhaps the killer would be so shocked, he or she would reveal themselves." Come to think of it, Katherine might just be desperate enough to try. Her playful demeanor sobered, and she stood straighter. "Do you think we might be able to bait the murderer into attacking me if I wore the ribbons?"

Lyle's expression darkened. "No. Don't think of it." His words were cutting, his tone absolute.

When she opened her mouth, he cut her off. "I mean it, Katherine. We will not bait the murderer, certainly not with you. Try it, and I'll arrest you, if that's what it takes to keep you safe."

She raised her hands in surrender. "Forget I mentioned it."

He scowled as he continued to lean against the wall, brooding.

To lighten the mood, Katherine teased, "Perhaps

I'll continue on with matchmaking once this party is through. Are you looking for a wife, Lyle?"

He shuddered and ran a hand through a hank of his ginger hair falling into his eyes. "You sound like my mother."

"She sounds like an intelligent woman."

"I am far too busy for romance. Feel free to pass that message on to her, since she doesn't seem to listen when I speak." He fiddled with his collar. "I spend half my time chasing down criminals and the other half creating easier ways to hunt criminals. You understand that, don't you?" He sounded a bit desperate.

Katherine took pity on him. "I do," she assured him as she reached out to pat his arm. "I was only teasing."

Fortunately, at that moment, Mrs. Burwick climbed up the stairs at last. Katherine dropped her arm and straightened, ready to confront her. When she noticed them lingering outside her door, Mrs. Burwick hesitated. For a moment, Katherine feared she would run. Lyle must have thought the same, for he tensed as if readying to run after her.

Instead, Mrs. Burwick donned an impassive expression and closed the distance between them. "Lady Katherine, to what do I owe this pleasure?" Her voice indicated that she derived no pleasure from this meeting at all.

"May we speak with you privately, Mrs. Burwick?"

The woman hesitated then nodded. Turning her back, she gestured them into her room and entered behind them. Once she shut the door, she turned to them with her back straight. Despite Katherine and Lyle's superior heights, Mrs. Burwick did not appear to be cowed. "What is this concerning?"

Katherine removed the ribbon from her reticule. "I found these in your room."

Mrs. Burwick bristled. "You have no right to search my room!"

"I have the leave of the host to do whatever I deem necessary to catch this murderer. Or did you forget that you were under the Earl of Northbrook's roof?"

The twitch of the older woman's eye betrayed her unease. "Those are ribbons. I don't know why you care to remark on them."

"They are *pink* ribbons," Katherine insisted. "Very similar to the one wrapped around Miss Young's throat last night."

If Katherine had hoped for an indication of Mrs. Burwick's guilt or innocence, she was destined to be disappointed. The older woman maintained her impenetrable composure, showing only a slight tinge of surprise. "It is not against the law to keep ribbons in one's room. I did not strangle Miss Young."

Lyle shifted in place, seeming impatient. *My goodness, was he inclined to believe Mrs. Burwick?* All murderers denied being caught if they wanted to live, and the woman still had high aspirations for her daughter.

"You hope for us to believe that you brought pink ribbon to a house party after the horrid fates of the last two young women clad in such a color?" Katherine stood arms akimbo. "Don't take us for fools, madam."

The older woman's shoulders slumped. "I didn't bring them. The Duke of Somerset gave them to me."

Katherine frowned. *Somerset? Why would he have pink ribbon? Why would he be giving ribbon to Mrs. Burwick?*

His voice every bit as authoritative as it had been last night when he'd sent the guests to bed, Lyle demanded, "Why would he do a thing like that?" When he acted in the capacity of Sir John's voice in society, the transformation was nothing short of miraculous. His absentminded inventor and investigator demeanor was gone. He could have gone toe to toe with Captain Wayland for who radiated the most authority.

Mrs. Burwick melted to his will like butter. Her

eyes downcast, she confessed, "I am in negotiations with him to make Prudence his next wife. He thought I had left the ribbons in his room while I was there. I tried to tell him he was mistaken, that they must belong to one of his... companions. However, we were interrupted, so I took the ribbons for the time being. I've never used them"—her gaze flicked toward Katherine—"for the very reasons you named. I don't want Pru to become the next victim."

She isn't blond. Katherine held her tongue as Lyle asked, "When did you receive the ribbons?"

"Yesterday, or perhaps the day before."

"Before the attack?"

"Yes." The woman's face hardened. "I didn't harm anyone. You must believe me."

If she had indeed been in negotiations with Lord Somerset, she stood to receive everything that she wanted. Why, then, would she attack Miss Young? Katherine remained silent as Lyle thanked Mrs. Burwick for her time and warned her not to conceal vital information in the future. They departed, taking the ribbons with them.

The moment they entered the corridor and shut the door, Lyle turned to Katherine. "We'll have to speak with the duke, to verify her tale."

"Of course. His room isn't far down the hall, so we can start there and check elsewhere if he isn't inside."

Lyle nodded, and they meandered toward the bachelors' end of the guest wing. "Do you think she's telling the truth?" he asked.

"Even if she is, Somerset might have kept a ribbon for himself if he planned something nefarious. But why attack Miss Young? Unless she openly spurned him in some way. She *is* more beautiful than Pru; perhaps the duke hoped to have her instead. And let's not forget our theory of a serial kill—"

A hoarse scream pierced the air from the other end of the guest wing, stopping Katherine and Lyle in their tracks. They exchanged a fearful glance.

Miss Young.

They bolted toward Miss Young's room.

CHAPTER TWENTY-ONE

When Katherine reached Miss Young's room, she found the door ajar and Mr. Greaves peering out the window. Miss Young moaned and shifted in bed. She was awake!

But why is Mr. Greaves in her room?

The moment Katherine stepped into the chamber, with Lyle on her heels, Mr. Greaves turned from the windowsill. The shutters were thrown wide, revealing the wan afternoon light, the sun hidden behind clouds. The curtain, still drawn and hastily stuffed to the side, fell in folds across Mr. Greaves's shoulder. When he stepped away from the window, the curtain fell into place once more, shutting out the light and dimming the room.

"You must hurry," he urged. "He jumped out the window!"

"Out of a two-story window?" Katherine glanced out and saw a trellis clinging to the house under the window. Roses reached halfway up. He could have shimmied down, but he couldn't have gone far. That was a heavy drop at the bottom. In fact, he might even have injured himself.

Katherine spared a quick glance toward Lyle before they split ways. He dashed to the window, throwing the drapes wide as he peered out in a manner identical to Mr. Greaves. Katherine hurried to Miss Young, hoping she wasn't further harmed. She took the rousing woman's clammy hand as she sat next to her on the bed. A pillow lay on the floor beside the bed.

Behind her, Lyle muttered, "No one is below. He's gotten away. Don't let anyone touch this windowsill. I'll return directly with my case." Katherine presumed he spoke to her, though he mumbled his words as he strode from the room.

Miss Young squeezed Katherine's hand, her eyes wide as she fully regained consciousness. She started to speak then moaned and clutched her throat.

"Hush, Miss Young," Katherine urged, keeping her voice low and gentle. "You're safe. I must learn what happened here, but I will stray no farther than the door. I spy a pitcher of water. Are you thirsty?"

Miss Young brushed her fingertips over her matted hair as she nodded. Once Katherine fetched her a glass and found that the woman was strong enough to sit up and drink from it without aid, she turned to the man left in the room.

Mr. Greaves, to his credit, had retreated nearer the door, possibly to avoid alarming Miss Young with his presence in her room. He shifted as if uncomfortable at remaining even there, under the circumstances. Katherine hailed him before he drifted too far and joined him on the threshold of the open door.

She kept her voice low as she approached him, lest Miss Young hear. "Why were you in Miss Young's chamber?"

He flashed her a smile, though this was not a time for levity. "I was on my way to my room when I heard her scream. I entered to see to her welfare. Tell me you would not have done the same, Lady Katherine."

Katherine most certainly would have, so she couldn't fault his answer even if it was unseemly for a gentleman to enter a lady's room. "You said you saw a man?" she asked, her tone brusque.

His smile slipped. "I don't know. The curtains were drawn, and it was dark in the room. When I burst in he was already halfway out the window. All I saw was a glimpse of the emerald-colored jacket he wore. I'm afraid I was too consumed with Miss Young's safety. By the time I rushed to the window, he was gone and you arrived."

Surviving that fall uninjured would take a true athlete—or a healthy dose of luck. Since neither Mr. Greaves nor Lyle had noticed anyone suspicious lurking below, the man in question must be a quick runner. Katherine had previously encountered the same swiftness from the man who ran from her in the gardens.

Katherine stifled a sigh. "You didn't see his face at all?"

Mr. Greaves shook his head.

"What of his height?"

"Near yours, Lady Katherine. Perhaps a bit taller or shorter."

In other words, the same height as every man in England. Well, all except for Lyle and Captain Wayland. Katherine waved her hand, dismissing Mr. Greaves. "I think it best if you vacate Miss Young's bedchamber, sir."

He inclined his head, the corner of his mouth twitching in annoyance. By the time he straightened, his smile had returned. "I'd like to assist the search in any way I can, Lady Katherine."

"If I need your assistance, I will find you. Thank you, Mr. Greaves."

As he turned away, Lyle returned and squeezed past him into the room. He paused and lowered his head to speak to Katherine in a low tone. "Did you discover anything else?"

"Nothing yet. I'm about to question Miss Young to hear her recollections."

When Katherine returned to Miss Young's side, the young woman warily eyed Lyle, who crossed to the windowsill. She gathered the sheets to her chest to better cover her. "Who is he?" she asked hoarsely. Her voice cracked, and it clearly pained her.

Katherine reclaimed the spot next to Miss Young's hip. "Pay him no mind. He is my friend, Mr. Murphy, with Sir John's men."

Her eyes widened. "A Bow Street Runner?"

Katherine nodded. "He and Lord Northbrook take this attack against you very seriously."

Miss Young licked her lips and stared into her glass but didn't say anything further.

Gently, Katherine prodded, "I know this is difficult and frightening for you, but I must ask. Yesterday in the garden, did you see who attacked you?"

The young woman's bloodshot eyes filled with tears. She looked down, her chin wobbling as her hands tightened around her glass. "I—" Her voice cracked again.

"Take your time. Anything you might be able to remember will help. I know it hurts to speak. Is the pain less if you whisper?"

"I don't know." Miss Young paused. She felt at her throat, sticky with the brownish paste the physician had prescribed to heal her bruises. "I do think it feels a bit better, but it is not at all pleasant."

"Would you like some more water?"

When Miss Young nodded, Katherine moved to refill her glass. The young woman drank half of the liquid before she spoke again.

"I didn't see who attacked me. Forgive me, I know I'm no help." She blinked hard against the moisture shining in her eyes.

"What *did* you see?"

"Little more than a man's shadow. He was upon me so quickly, I barely had time to scream. I never saw his face... I chose that darkened corner of the garden for a reason, so I wouldn't be found out when I..." She bit her lower lip.

Katherine leaned forward. "When you did what, precisely?"

The matted strands of Miss Young's hair fell

forward to shield her face, her cheeks pink with embarrassment or withheld tears. "I sent a note to Lord Northbrook. He's been paying me some attention, but he suddenly stopped. I hoped to continue our courtship in private. Do you think he—"

"He was in the parlor at the time." Or so Katherine had heard. Would the gathering lie for him because he was their host?

Miss Young finished the water in her glass and handed it to Katherine. When Katherine asked if she wanted it refilled, the young woman declined. Katherine set it aside next to the pitcher and returned.

"And this afternoon? Miss Young, when you awoke, you screamed. What did you see?"

The color drained from the young woman's face. Even her pale hair seemed dark by comparison. "I thought that was a nightmare." Her voice gained in strength. "I saw a man standing over me!"

"Did you see his face?" *Please tell me you did.*

"No. He held a pillow in front of him, and it was dim, and I was woozy. Mama!"

For a moment, Katherine frowned. As she glanced behind her to the door, she spotted Mrs. Young. The woman dashed to the bedside with tears in her eyes.

"Mama, I want to go home. I'm so afraid."

Mrs. Young wrenched Katherine away from her daughter. "Be gone! I won't have you harming my daughter."

Miss Young clutched her mother's wrist. "Lady Katherine hasn't harmed me. It was..." She scrunched her nose as her tears fell. "I don't know who, but he's certain to try to finish the job. Please, Mama. I don't care about finding a husband anymore. I only want to go home."

With a gaze as sharp as steel, Mrs. Young turned from Katherine to Lyle, who straightened from the windowsill. "She is the victim here. Surely you wouldn't keep us where she might be in danger."

"Of course not, madam. You and your daughter are free to go. Her matchmaker will have to stay, however."

His answer seemed to partially mollify the older woman. "Please, leave us. We must ready ourselves to leave at once." With that dismissal, she sat next to her daughter and hugged her tight.

Lyle beckoned Katherine closer. As she stepped near, she whispered, "Did you find anything?"

He pointed to the windowsill, where his powder had adhered to a mark. When he lifted a magnifying glass over it, the mark showed an intricate pattern of whorls interrupted by a thin line. He moved the magnifying glass to the pink ribbon, where the dye illuminated the same interrupted pattern.

"The attacker was certainly here."

Mr. Greaves had been telling the truth. All Katherine needed to find now was a man in an emerald-green jacket.

CHAPTER TWENTY-TWO

A cloud hung over the gathering. Even the dowager seemed shaken. She hid it well, keeping her back straight and her hands folded in her lap, but Katherine noticed the pronounced lines of worry around her nose and mouth. The hostess continually glanced around the room as if ensuring that all of her guests were present and safe. She contributed to the conversation on the settee with words as clipped as the melody Miss Reardon played on the pianoforte.

Katherine scanned the interior, pretending that she didn't notice the black glower aimed her way by Mrs. Fairchild. Fortunately, the rival matchmaker remained across the room, too far to drip her poison into Katherine's ear. She didn't appear to be taking the news of Miss Young's departure with grace, likely because it meant that she had been unsuccessful.

Where was Annie? Katherine had been so busy with Lyle all day as they uncovered clues that she hadn't had time to speak with her charge at all. When she was unable to find Annie's figure among the guests in the parlor, Katherine stopped Lady Reardon. "Have you seen Miss Pickering?"

The older woman shook her head. "I'm afraid not. She was at supper, I'm certain, but I haven't seen her since the gentlemen joined us here." Her gaze sharpened, and she leaned closer with a conspiratorial smile. "Is it true what they say, that you're working with the Bow Street Runner? What have you found?"

"I am not at liberty to discuss the investigation."

From the corner of her eye, Katherine spotted Captain Wayland as he extricated himself from a knot of gentlemen chatting by the mantel. His gaze fastened on her. By now, Katherine could read that particular expression as if he held a sign detailing his intentions. He meant to coax information from her.

It won't happen. Katherine was close to solving this case. Far too close to risk Wayland stealing the glory. She excused herself and briskly slipped away.

Instead of taking the main staircase up to the guest wing, she took the servants' stair. She didn't want Wayland to follow and corner her. She pressed her back against the wood-paneled wall and held her breath as she waited. At any moment, she expected him to peer around the corner and find her.

Silence. She was safe. Releasing a sigh of relief, she hurried up the stairs to the guest wing.

At the top, she heard voices. She pressed herself against the shadows again, craning her ears.

"Forgive me, Your Grace," said a woman, young by the sound of her voice. Katherine peered around the corner of the stairwell to spot a serving girl no older than twenty standing at the Duke of Somerset's door. Her face was pink and her eyes downcast. She fisted her hands in her skirts as she curtsied.

"You look familiar..." Katherine didn't stand at the proper angle to see into the doorway, but Somerset sounded amused.

Her color deepened. "I am Mrs. Fairchild's maid, Your Grace. We, erm... we met at your house party early this month." She plucked at her skirts, likely passed down from her employer. They were darned in places but neat.

"Ah, yes, I recall now. Would you like to come back later? I'm due down in the parlor with the other guests, but I'd love to entertain you afterward."

Katherine made a face but held her tongue as she continued to eavesdrop.

"This will only take a moment, Your Grace. I know

it is bold of me, but I must speak with you while my mistress is occupied. I... You see..." She brushed her cheeks. Was she crying? "If you'll forgive my crassness, I missed my courses this month. I've only ever lain with you. I was curious, you see, and you have so much experience on the matter that I..." She bit her lower lip. "When my mistress discovers I'm with child, she'll turn me out without a reference. Please, Your Grace, I beg you for a position in one of your households. I'm a hard worker..."

Lord Somerset stepped out of his room to lay his left arm around the young woman's shoulders. "I suppose I have a moment or two to spare. Come in, my dear, and we'll have a word about your future. If you are carrying my child, I assure you, you will both be well taken care of."

As he guided the maid into the room, Katherine stared at his sleeve, which was emerald green, the color that Mr. Greaves had described. Her heart trumpeted in her ears as she forced herself to breathe evenly. This was it, the answer for which she searched.

Somerset had motive—albeit a weak one—to exact revenge on the beautiful young debutantes who spurned the suit of a duke.

Apparently Mrs. Burwick had been telling the

truth about the ribbons. He'd had them in his room and had rid himself of them at precisely the right moment.

He'd injured his arm between the first and second murders, which might account for the reduction of violence in the subsequent crimes. Most importantly, he matched the description given of the man who had tried to murder Miss Young only that morning.

The latch to the door clicked, shutting Somerset in with the hapless young maid. Katherine couldn't confront him about any of this. She needed to find Lyle and present the evidence to force Somerset's confession. But first, she needed to check in with Annie to ask why she wasn't down with the other guests.

As Katherine passed Lord Somerset's door on the way to hers, doubts wiggled into her mind. She faltered and stared at the door.

Was he the murderer? He wouldn't dare harm a maid in the very room the host had allotted him—it would be far too brazen, even for a duke. And he'd acted most kindly to her and seemed dutiful toward his child. Could he be the same man that would callously murder Miss Rosehill and Miss Smythe, who was presumably also bearing his child?

Although he might have managed to overpower Miss Rosehill and Miss Young despite his injured arm, how had he managed to jump from a second-story window without injuring himself further? The man was in his seventies! She doubted he'd be able to shimmy down the trellis with that injured arm.

He'd told Mrs. Burwick the ribbons had been left in his room, but Katherine only had Mrs. Burwick's say-so on that. Might someone be attempting to frame him for the murders? Mrs. Burwick herself, perhaps, or even her daughter could be to blame. Katherine had never gotten a chance to search their rooms for fans that might be missing the chip of ivory. And *why* had Pru taken Miss Smythe's diary?

Something didn't add up. Katherine bit her lip and carried on. She entered her room, which Harriet was busy straightening. The adjoining door was ajar, so after greeting her maid, Katherine peered into Annie's room. She wasn't there.

Frowning, Katherine bent to greet Emma, who shamelessly begged for a rub. "Have you seen Annie?" she asked her friend.

"Not since I sent her down to supper," Harriet answered. "Why? Has she messed her hair again?"

"No. She isn't down with the guests." As Katherine straightened, she breathed deeply and evenly.

Don't panic. Annie must be somewhere on the grounds.

So must the Pink-Ribbon Killer, who had just been denied a victim earlier that day... and even though Annie wasn't blond, perhaps the killer was getting desperate. That was, *if* the killer was killing simply to satisfy his urges rather than having a purpose. No matter the reason, she wasn't about to risk Annie's life.

Harriet seemed to share Katherine's alarm. She straightened from her task on the vanity, clutching a small box in her hand. "You don't think..."

"I'll search the premises."

"I'll help." She moved to set down the box then frowned at it. "Where did you get this, Lady Katherine?"

With all the excitement, she'd forgotten to return Mowbry's snuffbox. She accepted it from her maid. "It isn't mine. I don't have time to return it now, not until I discover where Annie has run off to. Will you search the house? I'll start in the garden."

"Of course."

"If you happen to see Lyle, please ask him to search as well. Perhaps I'm jumping to conclusions, but I must find Annie first."

They parted ways, Katherine leaving her dog with

Harriet as she hurried down the main steps to the ground floor. She dashed for the nearest exit.

Gathering her skirts, Katherine stepped outside and swiftly made her way to the garden path. If Annie was innocently outdoors, she would likely be searching for another moth. Katherine began her search at the same area of the garden where Annie had found the yellow-bellied moth—or whatever it was called—the first time around.

As she approached the area, she heard voices. Slowing, she peeked around the nearest corner to espy the speakers. That had certainly been Annie's voice, and she didn't seem in the best of spirits. Was Annie in danger?

When Katherine peeked around the corner to assess the situation, she was glad for her forethought in looking before she leaped. Lord Northbrook took a step nearer to Annie, closing the distance between them. He cupped her chin and tipped it up to meet his gaze. "Don't be disappointed, Miss Pickering."

"How can I not be? That violet-banded elephant moth was such a rare find! It would have been the perfect addition to my collection. I've never seen one like it outside a book before."

A slow smile spread across Northbrook's lips as he

bent to kiss her. Annie gasped a second before his lips made contact, then she melted into his embrace.

When he lifted his head, he said, "I know a way you can add that moth to your collection."

Annie seemed disoriented as she blinked up at him. "How?"

His smile grew. "By becoming my wife."

Grinning to herself, Katherine bit her lip and retreated to leave them in their private moment. Somehow, her matchmaking job had worked itself aright, after all. Now, if only she could find the Pink-Ribbon Killer, all would be perfect.

Since Annie was under Northbrook's watchful eye, Katherine had no qualms about leaving her in the garden. The earl would ensure her safety. As Katherine strolled back to the manor to alert Harriet and Lyle that she had been successful in finding Annie, her mind was free of concerns regarding her charge. Her thoughts turned to the murders.

Did the Duke of Somerset truly find the ribbons in his room, or had Mrs. Burwick made that up? Since he wasn't a woman and therefore didn't wear them, they were bound to be out of place. The only reason someone might put the ribbons where they were certain to be found would be to ensure that Somerset was arrested for the murders.

However, Mrs. Burwick might have lied about the origin of the ribbons. She had ample motive to want to further her daughter's marriage prospects, which was not to mention Pru continually turning up in odd locations. She searched for something in Lord Northbrook's chambers, and she'd even stolen Miss Smythe's diary.

What possible motive could she have for doing so, unless she'd known that she might in some way have been mentioned in the pages? When Katherine had skimmed the diary, having precious little time with it, she had only searched for mentions of the men in Miss Smythe's life as she attempted to discern who might have been the father of her child.

Miss Young had said a man tried to strangle her. Pru was no dainty flower. Could she have disguised herself as a man?

Perhaps the ivory chip that had been found at Miss Rosehill's murder had been dislodged from Pru's fan as she strangled Miss Rosehill. After all, the victim was especially close with Pru, and in fact had grown distant from her for some unknown reason.

As she turned the corner, the manor door in view, a fly separated from the shuttered lamp at the entrance to the garden. Katherine swatted at it as it buzzed around her head. Her reticule thumped against her wrist painfully. She tried to remember what she had put in there.

Oh, yes. The snuffbox. Lest she manage to bruise herself, Katherine removed the box from her reticule. As she did, her fingertips grazed the rough edges of the lid.

The *ivory* lid. She lifted it to examine it more closely. Although many of the chips were yellowed with age, one particular triangular corner showed white, bright ivory. If Katherine checked Lyle's notebook for the shape he'd traced, she was willing to wager that it would match the box. The chip hadn't come from a woman's fan at all. It had been from this snuffbox.

Her heart skipped. Mowbry was the killer, just as she'd originally suspected.

Perhaps his claim that he didn't care about Miss Smythe becoming pregnant with another man's baby was not true. He would have known Katherine had read about the pregnancy in the diary and would have been compelled to make it seem like it didn't matter lest it make her suspicious of him. Had he killed Miss Smythe when he found out? Miss Smythe and Miss Rosehill had been friends, so it was possible that Rosehill had suspected Mowbry was the killer and confronted him, at which point he killed her so she couldn't tell anyone.

But that didn't explain the attempt on Miss Young.

Maybe Mowbry decided that killing suited him. His boots matched the footprint, and Greaves mentioned that he'd been worried or looking for Mowbry that night. She wasn't sure if Mowbry had a green jacket, but he was young and could easily jump out the window and shimmy down the trellis of Miss Young's room.

At the society meeting, Phil had said to get the proof and use it to cause the killer to confess, and this snuffbox was the proof.

She clutched the box in her hand and ran back to the house. She needed to corner Mowbry and make sure he didn't escape. He must be getting nervous, now that Lyle was on the case. And she needed to get Lyle's notebook, to compare the chip and use that proof to gain a confession.

Rushing inside, she ignored the narrow-eyed glances of Mrs. Fairchild and Mrs. Burwick. Lord Mowbry wasn't in the parlor. Should she seek Lyle out first?

She was heading toward the stairs when she spotted Mr. Greaves.

"Lady Katherine, is something amiss?" Greaves glanced down at the snuffbox and frowned.

Katherine tightened her fist over the box, the rough chip digging into her palm. If anyone, Mr. Greaves would know where Lord Mowbry was. "Have you seen Lord Mowbry?"

"You seem flustered. Is there something I can help with?" Mr. Greaves crossed his arms over his chest. Was he covering for his friend?

"It's vital I find him at once."

Mr. Greaves stared at her for a few seconds then nodded. "Very well, I believe he is in the grotto." Greaves leaned closer to her, a slight smile on his lips. "Possibly entertaining Miss Reardon."

Katherine's heart jerked in her chest. Mowbry was going to kill again!

She didn't have time to look for Lyle. Miss Reardon could be in danger, and she was not about to let another young woman get harmed because she wasn't there to help. She turned on her heel and ran out to the garden.

CHAPTER TWENTY-THREE

The grotto was empty. *Where has Lord Mowbry taken Miss Reardon?*

She hurried along, looking in the various alcoves where she knew there were benches. Nothing.

Had he taken her off the premises to kill her?

The snuffbox grew heavy in her hand. She looked down at it. Why hadn't she been convinced of Mowbry's guilt sooner? She might have prevented this. But his pain about Miss Smythe's death had seemed so sincere, and in her diary she'd sounded so sure that he had accepted her even in her delicate condition.

Her thoughts drifted back to the conversation she'd had with Mowbry when she'd found him drinking, as if that might hold a clue as to where he would have taken Miss Reardon. She could have sworn the man was genuinely distraught.

Then Mr. Greaves had come in that night. What had Mowbry called him? Monty, a nickname for the old family name of Montrose. She looked down at the snuffbox with the monogrammed "*M*" on it again, and everything clicked into place.

Greaves had been in Miss Young's room when someone had tried to suffocate her. Greaves had injured his thumb when he'd been admiring the roses in the garden. The imprint of his finger had been on the ribbon. And it had been on Miss Young's windowsill because he had touched it as he looked out. He'd not seen another man jumping out of the window —he'd been cleverly covering for his own presence in the room.

And, come to think of it, Greaves had fingered Lord Somerset at every turn. And confound it, he even had the same size foot as Lord Mowbry—he'd asked Mowbry if he could borrow his riding boots!

She'd been wrong... oh so wrong. She needed to get back to the house quickly.

But before she could turn and run, a hand crushed over her mouth and nose, stopping her in her tracks and jerking her back into the grotto.

CHAPTER TWENTY-FOUR

Katherine couldn't breathe. Her mouth tasted salty and metallic. With the man's pinky holding her chin closed and her nose pinched closed beneath his thumb and palm, she couldn't draw even a tendril of air. She thrashed, but his arm around her middle pinned her arms to her side. Her heels dragged along the path as he pulled her away from the lantern and deeper into the grotto.

She refused to go quietly. Katherine struggled to kick her heels. However, they were matched in height, which didn't leave her with a lot of room. When she stomped on his foot with all of her weight, he cursed but faltered for no more than a moment. Continuing to fight made her head swim. Her lungs ached. She needed a breath.

If he thought her dead or unconscious, he might

remove his hand. Katherine fell limp against him, fighting all her instincts, given the burning in her lungs and throat from lack of air. Tears leaked from the corners of her eyes. *Please, let this not be a mistake.* Her attacker stilled a moment, wavering beneath her weight. Then, blessed be, his hand shifted as he continued to drag her.

It took every iota of Katherine's willpower not to gulp in air like a starving man devouring a meal. As she breathed in through her nose in shallow pants that only marginally appeased the ache in her chest, her head continued to spin. She didn't have to pretend to fall limp; in fact, it would have been more of a challenge to hold her own weight. Her ears rang as her attacker dragged her away.

Distantly, she heard another sound. When she opened her eyes the barest sliver, her blurred vision picked out the bob of a lantern. As the ringing started to subside, she could hear voices laughing and intimate. She recognized Annie's tone at once.

Find me. Help.

The man dragged her behind the corner of the manse, out of sight, a mere heartbeat before the light would have reached them. He dropped her onto the soggy ground, moist from recent rain. As she hit, what meager breath she'd managed to draw gushed from between her lips in a grunt and an audible whoosh. No doubt he knew her to be awake after that. She opened her eyes in time for the light to illuminate her attacker's profile.

Mr. Greaves.

Shakily, Katherine drew herself into a sitting position and guzzled in air. The spinning in her head lessened with every breath, allowing her to think. Unfortunately, none of her thoughts were optimistic. Her knees were as weak as watered-down wine. If she tried to run, he would be on her in an instant. She had to buy herself time to recover.

She had to keep him talking. What better way to do that than by having him confess? What was it Phil had advised? Katherine breathed deeply as she searched her foggy mind.

Catch him in the act.

Well, there was no better time than now, when he'd attacked her. After this, he wouldn't emerge unscathed. She had him caught, to be sure, if she managed to emerge from this alive.

To encourage him to talk, she asked, "Why? Why do this?"

A sneer painting his mouth, he bent to pick up something she'd dropped—the snuffbox. He rubbed his thumb across it as if checking for new chips before he stuffed the box into his pocket. In its place, he pulled out a ribbon.

Remain calm. So long as she remained calm and encouraged him to talk, she could regain enough strength to run. Lyle and Harriet searched the manor, and when they found Annie, they would search next for her. Katherine had to remain calm and buy herself more time. If it came down to a struggle, would Katherine prevail over Mr. Greaves's strength? Perhaps at her full strength, when she didn't shake so much. She focused on her breathing and calming her hammering heart.

Mr. Greaves stepped forward into the shadows of the manor, out of the reach of the lantern at the entrance to the garden. His tone betrayed his disdain.

"I hadn't expected Miss Young to rouse, let alone scream. A seventy-year-old man hopping out a second-story window? I knew you'd see through that claim sooner or later. If you hadn't been attached to that sodding Bow Street Runner all day, you would have gotten what you deserve that much sooner."

He started to crouch while he advanced, and Katherine scurried back. Her elbows and knees threatened to collapse under the strain of motion. She didn't have the strength for a fight. She could scream now, but then she'd never get her confession, nor was she sure anyone would reach her before Greaves finished her off and ran.

"Not that," she bit off quickly. "I expected that. But why Miss Young? She's barely spoken to you."

He must have expected a different reaction, for he rocked back on his heels. Perhaps he waited for her to beg for her life. She wouldn't. She had more pride and fight than that.

She added, "You might as well tell me, if you mean to kill me. I'd rather not go to my death with this mystery left unfinished."

He chuckled. "You weren't clever enough to puzzle it out in time, were you?" Slowly straightening to tower above her once more, Mr. Greaves answered in a bored tone. "Miss Young had the misfortune of being a silly girl without the sense to remain with her chaperone."

"So she was in the wrong place at the wrong time?"

"And she resembled the wrong woman."

So Katherine had been right to suspect that connection, after all. "This is all about Miss Smythe."

"Isobel." He bit off the name like poison. "Yes. That unfaithful cow got what she deserved. The others... well, someone had to be brought to justice for the killings. Why not Somerset? He has one foot in the grave anyway. Not to mention he is halfway to senile and conveniently missing from the gathering most of the time. I even saw him sneak off with a maid when I let myself into his garden to meet with Isobel that fateful evening."

Katherine pushed herself into a sitting position, testing her weight on her arms. They trembled but not as severely as a minute before. Her head was clearer, as well. "You've been trying to frame the Duke of Somerset."

"Trying," he scoffed, taking a step nearer. "I would have succeeded if not for my hasty lie this morning. Once you bothered to look, you would have found the ribbons in his room." He laughed. "I thought you had me caught for a minute the other day when I came out, but I suppose you had your little mind too focused on marriage prospects. A stroke of luck, wouldn't you say?"

Katherine cringed at her lapse. If only she'd counted the doors properly that day. Lord Somerset and Lady Burwick had both been telling the truth about the ribbons. Greaves had planted them.

Now she remembered that the bust of Caesar was in between Lord Somerset and Lady Reardon's room, but when she'd seen Greaves, she had been just past the bust, heading into the section for the married chambers. Greaves had come out of the room on the other side of the bust, which was Lord Somerset's room, not Mrs. Reardon's as she'd assumed. She shifted her legs a bit to try to get her heels beneath her. She moved slowly, so as not to arouse his suspicions. "And in the garden when you confessed you'd heard Somerset threaten Miss Rosehill, was that a lie?"

Greaves nodded.

"I don't understand. Why Miss Smythe? If you were trying to protect your friend Mowbry, why not simply warn him that she was intimate with another man?"

Bones popped, as if Mr. Greaves clenched his fists so hard that he cracked his knuckles. Katherine froze, fearing that she would prod him into attacking her and finishing the deed.

"Miss Smythe," he spat, "deserved what came to her for her lies. That little adventuress pretended that she was different from all the other rapacious debutantes. She was bedding me the entire time she made eyes at Mowbry. Then she has the audacity to tell me our affair was over because she *fell in love* and intended to marry my closest friend? I couldn't let that rest."

"So you killed her?"

"My temper got away from me, I'll admit, but it

ended up for the best. Mowbry and I—we're both better off without her." He stepped closer. "And I'm afraid the gathering will be better off without you prying into everyone's business, *Lady* Katherine."

Not yet. She scurried away from him on still-watery knees. To keep him talking, she said the first thing that jumped to her mind. "Don't you care about the grief you've caused your closest friend?"

Mr. Greaves hesitated. "Grief? I've done him a favor."

"You've left him heartbroken. Certainly, he covers it by flirting—"

"As he should."

Katherine got her heels beneath her. She braced one palm against the wall, hoping Mr. Greaves could see as little as she. Her only hope of surviving was to run when the moment was ripe.

The scoundrel added, "The only way to get over the wounded pride left by a woman is to find another. I encouraged Mowbry to return to sowing his wild oats. Forget about the little whore who would have cuck-olded him, given the chance."

Slowly, Katherine moved from sitting to a squat. Her legs wobbled, but she couldn't keep him talking for much longer. She had to make her escape as soon as she could muster the strength.

"Is that what you did?" The suggestion turned her stomach, but it did as she expected and distracted him.

His voice warmed as he stepped forward. Whether by design or luck, he stepped on her hem, effectively trapping her. *Sard these infernal skirts!*

"That is precisely what I did. At first it was just so I could frame Somerset. I needed to stage the murders better than Isobel's. But the entire time Miss Rosehill thrashed in my arms, I was thinking of Isobel. You don't look quite enough like her to satisfy—"

Crack!

Katherine gasped as Mr. Greaves reeled to the side. His head smacked against the stone bench before he fell to the ground. Another figure stood behind him, hefting an object. A woman?

"That's for killing my closest friend, you monster!"

Katherine tugged her hem from beneath Mr. Greaves's limp body. "Pru?"

Her savior stepped over the unconscious man to offer Katherine her hand. She helped Katherine stand. "Did he harm you?"

"Nothing lasting. I... Thank you, but I must ask, how did you find us?"

"I followed his steps. I was a bit delayed by Lord Northbrook as he returned from the garden, and wasn't certain which path you'd taken. I..." She fiddled with the object in her hand. "Oh, piddle. That knock over the head must have tipped out the oil."

It seemed an unlit lantern had been Mr. Greaves's undoing.

Katherine managed to keep her feet, feeling steadier with each passing moment. Swallowing against a knot of fear, she used the wall for support as she bent to find the ribbon Mr. Greaves had meant to use to strangle her. Her fingers trembled as she gripped it. She used it to truss him up instead, lest he regain consciousness.

"Oh, wait," Pru exclaimed. "I think I have it!" A spark flared to life, followed by a flame and a growing light in the lantern. Triumphant, she set it at Mr. Greaves's feet.

Gingerly, Katherine turned him over, curious to see whether he was dead or merely incapacitated. He seemed to be alive, though a gash in his head bled profusely. She stood and turned to face the other woman.

Pru wore a look of contempt as she beheld him. Katherine stepped closer and took her arm, leading her a few steps away from the scene, just as much for Katherine's peace of mind as for Pru's. "You said you followed him. Why?"

Pru pulled away and crossed her arms. Her mouth

remained mulish as she trained her eye upon Mr. Greaves. "I suspected all along that he killed my friends, Isobel and Mary—Miss Smythe and Miss Rosehill. I will never forgive him for taking them away." Tears gathered in her eyes, but she didn't bother to wipe them. In fact, they seemed to fuel her.

Katherine rubbed her shoulder. "Nor should you. But how did you learn it was him?"

"The diary. Mary and I had a falling out because she started seeing a man privately so soon after Isobel's murder. From various comments she made, I suspected it might be the father of Isobel's child, but I had no idea who it was. She said this was her one great romance before settling down. I told her it was her folly. If I'd only been more supportive, maybe she—" Pru paused to wipe her eyes. "She wouldn't tell me his name, and we shared everything, but I had my suspicions. After Isobel was killed, I talked Mama into hosting a party so I could try to figure out who killed her, and Mary ended up being killed at the party. It's all my fault. If I'd only figured it out sooner... Isobel's diary told me enough to put the lingering pieces together. When I noticed Mr. Greaves slip away from the parlor, I followed, hoping to catch him unawares. I was nearly too late again."

"You arrived at precisely the right time, Miss

Burwick." Katherine studied the girl. "So that's why you were in Mowbry's room and Northbrook's room? Looking for evidence?"

Pru nodded. The woman's hardened exterior cracked, and a smile slipped through. When smiling, with tears shining in her eyes, she looked approachable. Perhaps even beautiful. This entire time, Katherine had suspected her of having a heinous character, when in fact she had been working through her grief to find her friend's killer. Would Katherine have been able to think clearly, under the circumstances?

"Pru, please," the woman corrected.

Katherine smiled. "You know, Pru, I think you'd be a remarkable investigator, if you ever put your mind to it."

Her smile slipping, the other woman looked down. "I had extraordinary incentive, in this case. I won't rest until I see him brought to justice."

"So he will be. That, I can promise you."

CHAPTER TWENTY-FIVE

"I don't think the ribbon will hold him," Lyle mused as he stood over the unconscious body, examining it. "Well done on the lump on his head, though. He'll have a screeching headache for certain when he rouses."

Pru turned pink and lowered her gaze modestly.

Katherine, still a bit dazed, ceded the criminal to Lyle without comment. Harriet left the group to fetch a stronger rope to keep the man bound for the duration of the journey to London.

As she departed, Wayland stepped around the corner of the manor. Katherine stifled a groan. Her chest still ached from her altercation with Mr. Greaves. She didn't have the fortitude to do battle with the rival detective at that moment.

Clasping his hands behind his back, Wayland

stepped up next to her. He surveyed the unconscious man as Lyle unknotted the ribbon from around his wrists.

"You found him. Allow me to tender my congratulations on a job well done."

Katherine eyed him warily. "That's all you mean to say? Congratulations?"

He smirked but hid it behind his broad palm as he rubbed one hand over his chin. When he returned his hand to his side, he looked composed once more. "Did you expect something different?"

"A reminder that we might have worked more quickly together, perhaps."

"It seems to me that you already know that. Perhaps when our paths cross again, you'd do well to remember that we are on the same side."

Katherine didn't have anything further to say. She turned away, locking her knees to keep from leaning her weight against the solid, welcoming wall. After the excitement of the evening, she wanted nothing more than to retire to bed.

Wayland asked, "Are you certain he is at fault?"

"I *am* certain. He made a full confession."

"What did he say, precisely?"

Annoyed, Katherine shot him a glare. He didn't seem the least bit moved by her open hostility. "I've already given a full account to Lyle, who will be accompanying Mr. Greaves to London."

"Alone, with a burly chap like him?" Wayland shook his head. "I won't hear of it. We can't have Mr. Greaves escaping custody. Mr. Murphy, please accept my assistance in escorting our prisoner to London. We can take my carriage, if you haven't one."

Lyle hesitated. He glanced at Katherine and drew out his words as he answered. "Your assistance would be welcome..."

Katherine stifled a sigh. She couldn't blame Lyle for wanting another body nearby to aid in the transport. Katherine couldn't provide such a service, for she remained Annie's chaperone until the conclusion of the party. With the murders solved, she hoped that everyone would disband and return home.

Wayland turned a dazzling smile upon her. "You see? If I'm to be escorting Mr. Greaves, I ought to know all the information at hand in case I have to give a report."

"Why don't you ask Lyle?" she countered, her voice so falsely sweet it made her teeth ache. She turned to Pru, who looked every bit as weary as Katherine felt. "Why don't we return indoors and inform the party of this most welcome outcome to recent events?"

Nodding, the other woman stepped forward and linked her arm with Katherine's. "Yes, let's." As they strode toward the manor door, no one protested. The moment they turned the corner, Pru leaned closer and whispered, "Perhaps we should stop by my room first, however. I have something that doesn't belong to me."

By the time they reached the parlor, the room was abuzz with the news that *something* had happened, even if the occupants seemed too confused and on edge to have been informed of the details. As Katherine and Pru stepped into the room, a hush fell over those gathered. Everyone turned to stare at them with expressions of concern and curiosity.

Katherine drew herself up and announced, "Mr. Murphy, the representative of Sir John, has made an arrest. Mr. Greaves has confessed to the murders of Miss Smythe and Miss Rosehill, as well as the attack on Miss Young." *And on me.*

Gasps fluttered around the room like birds erupting into flight. The sounds were followed by mutters. Although Katherine could make out precious little with everyone speaking over each other, the consensus seemed to be that everyone had expected it all along.

She gritted her teeth. *This is the last time I'll have to find myself among these grasping, bacon-brained vultures.* They would have turned an ill opinion on anyone, for any perceived slight.

The person most affected by this news was Lord Mowbry. The color drained from his cheeks, and he sat heavily in the nearest armchair. "It can't be."

The whispers ceased, and the guests stared at him.

He rubbed a hand over his face. "Not Isobel—why would he?" When he glanced up, he seemed so forlorn that Katherine's heart broke for him. His best friend had killed the woman he loved. There were no words she could utter to soothe that situation.

"He wanted Miss Smythe for himself. I'm sorry."

Mowbry looked lost.

Clearing her throat, Pru stepped closer and offered him the journal in her hands. "I believe this belongs to you, now. To remember her by. She loved you."

When he met her gaze, his eyes shone with tears. "Thank you, Miss Burwick." His voice cracked as he reached for the journal.

The hush over the guests as they witnessed his pain seemed to deepen and writhe like a living thing. After glancing at Annie, Lord Northbrook cleared his throat.

"I have some news of my own that bears an announcement."

Everyone looked to him, including Katherine. At

his side, Annie ducked her head, her cheeks turning pink and her dimples winking to life as she tried to contain a smile.

Northbrook straightened his shoulders and reached for Annie's hand, which she gave him willingly. "I have asked Miss Pickering to be my wife, and she has accepted."

Exclamations encircled the room. Some—like Mrs. Fairchild's, "You cannot be serious!"—expressed surprise and disbelief. Others, mostly the men, conveyed their sincere congratulations for the happy news.

One sharp voice shattered them all to silence. "*Her?*"

Annie shrunk into Lord Northbrook's shadow as his mother elbowed her way between two matrons to stand in front of him. His expression didn't falter for a moment, nor did he release Annie's hand.

"Yes, Mother. I have fallen madly and deeply in love with this woman. She is beautiful and kind, energetic and intelligent. Best of all, she also collects moths and understands my interest in them."

Annie beamed, peeking around Northbrook's side. "Not only moths. I collect butterflies, as well. Some dragonflies. And—"

To Katherine's astonishment, the dowager started

to laugh. Her chuckle turned into a roaring guffaw that brought tears to her eyes. She wiped them, shaking her head as she muttered about Northbrook and his "bloody moths."

Smiling, she opened her arms and embraced Annie. "If he's found someone to make him this happy, you must be a gem, indeed."

Annie, although shocked, returned the embrace after a moment's hesitation.

The party descended on them, offering their congratulations to the engaged couple and to Katherine as well for a job well done. Katherine tried to protest—after all, she hadn't done much at all to facilitate this match, and she certainly didn't want to encourage future matchmaking requests—but her words fell on deaf ears. Between the swarm of matrons and debutantes who seemed bent on currying her favor, Katherine glimpsed Mrs. Fairchild seething in the corner of the room.

When Pru stepped in, trying to pry the throng away from Katherine, all she managed to do was make way for her own mother to step closer.

"What a brilliant coup you made with Miss Pickering," Mrs. Burwick exclaimed.

"It wasn't my doing. Miss Pickering is a lovely

young woman with plenty of assets to draw a man's eye—"

Mrs. Burwick slipped her arm through Katherine's and tugged her down until their heads were on the same level. "That little thing I told you regarding the Duke of Somerset seems to have fallen through. You don't think you might be able to orchestrate a match for my dear Prudence, do you?"

Pru turned a stark shade of white. She shook her head vigorous, silently begging Katherine to refuse.

Lucky for Pru, Katherine never intended to accept another matchmaking job. After all, she had set out to do precisely what she'd done. She'd solved a murder that even her father couldn't. Even if she had had some help in the end, her success spoke for itself.

When Papa learned of it, he would have to award her dowry as agreed. She had brought the Pink-Ribbon Killer to justice.

S eptember 1, 1816.
　　Katherine's twenty-fifth birthday.

KATHERINE'S BROWS tugged together as she skimmed the news rag. There, below a story of a string of robberies in Bath, was the account of the capture of the Pink-Ribbon Killer, which curiously named Lyle Murphy as the detective who had solved the crime. Wayland hadn't taken credit?

Katherine tossed the news rag at the table next to her. Seated in her father's study in front of the crackling fire in the hearth, she sighed as she leaned back into the overstuffed armchair. "Wayland must be up to something. He didn't take credit for capturing the

Pink-Ribbon Killer. I would think he would have pressed for credit so he could be paid." Katherine pursed her lips. Just who *had* hired Wayland to find the killer? Mowbry?

Papa leaned forward and patted her knee. His wry smile stretched across his square jaw. His blue-gray eyes twinkled. "Curious, isn't it? But then I was under the impression you caught the killer without help."

She bolted upright. "I did, Papa, I promise. I *didn't* accept his help, nor did he lift a finger to help me solve that case."

Papa raised his hand, ending her tirade. "I know. I asked your friend Lyle earlier when he arrived to wish you a happy birthday."

Katherine gnawed on her lower lip. Papa hadn't spoken a word of whether or not she had earned her dowry, stating that he would tell her once he had reviewed her work. Even though it might jeopardize the prize she so craved, she couldn't lie to him.

"In truth, Lyle did help me solve the murders. There was an attack while I was at Northbrook's estate, and I thought it more prudent to solve the matter quickly before someone else was hurt than to do it entirely on my own." She held her breath as she waited for his response.

After running his palm over his thinning pate,

Papa said, "I know, Katherine. You have a good heart. You've done well."

The air gushed from between her lips on a sigh. "I won the wager?"

"You did. Even the best of detectives must ask for help. In fact, I must insist that you keep someone like Lyle near at hand in order to minimize the danger to yourself. I don't know what I'd do without you, my dear."

Katherine smiled, her throat thick with emotion. *I love you too, Papa.* "I promise I'll take better care next time."

"Good." He nodded sternly. "Though I'll warn you of seeking Wayland's counsel in the future."

Katherine made a face as she stared at that mistrustful news article. "Trust me, I've learned that well enough."

Papa dipped his hand into the pocket of his blue waistcoat and removed a neatly pressed envelope. He handed it to her. "Happy birthday, darling. Once you present this at the bank, you'll have full control over your fortune."

Her hand trembling, she accepted the envelope. A lump grew in her throat, and she battled tears. "This is it. I'll never have to take another matchmaking job."

"But you must."

Her smile slipped as she met his shrewd gaze. "What? No, from this day forward, I'm an investigator, not a matchmaker!"

"There is quite the stigma attached to our profession, Katherine. If you openly proclaim your purpose, you'll find doors shut in your face. No, keep the matchmaking business. You're well established, and it will provide the perfect excuse for you to investigate wherever you please. Not to mention, with a business such as that, the other detectives at the Royal Society of Investigative Techniques will be free to seek you out, should they have information for you or need your opinion. You won't need to wait for the monthly meeting."

Katherine groaned as she acknowledged his point. "But Papa, with my recent success with Annie, the breadth of the *ton* will be pounding at my door to match up their daughters! When will I find the time to solve crime?"

With a fond smile, he patted her knee. "With a passion like yours, I'm certain you'll find the time."

A knock at the door interrupted the intimate moment. Katherine turned as Harriet opened it. Her gaze twinkled with mischief.

"Lady Katherine, you have visitors."

Papa stood. "See them in, Harriet. I'll show myself out for a moment."

Jumping to her feet, Katherine protested, "But Papa, this is your study!"

The earl leaned closer to kiss her cheek. "You'll have your own study soon enough, pumpkin. Until then, I'm happy to let you use mine. Come down to the parlor once you're through, and we'll celebrate with your sisters."

As he let himself out, Harriet showed in Mrs. Burwick and Pru. Katherine's stomach sank upon seeing them. Pru cast her an apologetic grimace and applied herself to examining the room as her mother bustled closer.

"Lady Katherine, how wonderful to see you again. Might we sit down?"

When Katherine smiled, it felt brittle. She hoped she at least gave the veneer of civility. "If you'll forgive my rudeness, I have a family engagement I must attend. May I ask why you're here?"

"Why, to further our conversation from the Earl of Northbrook's estate! I simply must secure your services for Prudence before you're deluged by other offers."

Pru looked as though she'd swallowed a lemon. She took a healthy step away from her mother as if hoping to separate herself from that line of inquiry as well. Katherine could well understand her reticence to marry, because Katherine shared it, hence why she had taken pains to secure her dowry for her own use.

While Pru craned her neck to read the news rag Katherine had tossed onto the table between the two armchairs, Katherine turned her attention to Mrs. Burwick. When she opened her mouth, prepared to turn her down—or, at the very least, delay her answer—the older woman interrupted her.

"I have just the lord in mind for my Prudence, and I have it on good authority that he means to holiday in Bath for the month of September."

Bath? That caught both Katherine and Pru's attention. Her lips pursed, Pru pointed to the news rag and cocked an eyebrow. Her eyes gleamed, an expression no doubt mirrored in Katherine. If she accepted this job, it would provide them with just the excuse they needed to venture to Bath to solve that murder.

As she opened her mouth, Mrs. Burwick cut her off again. "Money is no object, Lady Katherine. Whatever your fee, we will pay, so long as you promise to secure Prudence's future happiness."

Katherine and Pru shared a secret smile. Clearly Pru wanted no match, which would leave Katherine free to investigate the burglaries in Bath. And at the same time, she could help Pru make sure she didn't end up with a husband she didn't want. And *that* would secure Pru's future happiness, just as Mrs. Burwick wanted. As matchmaking jobs went, it was nearly perfect.

"Mrs. Burwick, how could I possibly say no to a friend?"

****

IF YOU LIKED THIS BOOK, you might also like my Hazel Martin Mystery series set in 1920s England:

Murder at Lowry House (book 1)
Murder by Misunderstanding (book 2)

SIGN UP TO join my email list to get all my latest release at the lowest possible price, plus as a benefit for signing up today, I will send you a copy of a Leighann Dobbs book that hasn't been published anywhere...yet!

http://www.leighanndobbs.com/newsletter

IF YOU ARE ON FACEBOOK, please join my VIP readers group and get exclusive content plus updates on all my books. It's a fun group where you can feel at home, ask questions and talk about your favorite reads:

https://www.facebook.com/groups/ldobbsreaders/

IF YOU WANT to receive a text message on your cell phone when I have a new release, text COZYMYS-TERY to 88202 (sorry, this only works for US cell phones!)

ALSO BY LEIGHANN DOBBS

Cozy Mysteries

Hazel Martin Historical Mystery Series

***

Murder at Lowry House (book 1)

Murder by Misunderstanding (book 2)

Lady Katherine Regency Mysteries

***

An Invitation to Murder (Book 1)

Sam Mason Mysteries

(As L. A. Dobbs)

***

Telling Lies (Book 1)

Keeping Secrets (Book 2)

Exposing Truths (Book 3)

Mooseamuck Island Cozy Mystery Series

* * *

A Zen For Murder

A Crabby Killer

A Treacherous Treasure

Lexy Baker Cozy Mystery Series

* * *

Lexy Baker Cozy Mystery Series Boxed Set Vol 1 (Books 1-4)

Or buy the books separately:

Killer Cupcakes

Dying For Danish

Murder, Money and Marzipan

3 *Bodies and a Biscotti*

Brownies, Bodies & Bad Guys

Bake, Battle & Roll

Wedded Blintz

Scones, Skulls & Scams

Ice Cream Murder

Mummified Meringues

Brutal Brulee (Novella)

No Scone Unturned

Cream Puff Killer

Silver Hollow

Paranormal Cozy Mystery Series

***

A Spell of Trouble (Book 1)

Spell Disaster (Book 2)

Nothing to Croak About (Book 3)

Cry Wolf (Book 4)

Mystic Notch

Cat Cozy Mystery Series

* * *

Ghostly Paws

A Spirited Tail

A Mew To A Kill

Paws and Effect

Probable Paws

Blackmoore Sisters

Cozy Mystery Series

* * *

Dead Wrong

Dead & Buried

Dead Tide

Buried Secrets

Deadly Intentions

A Grave Mistake

Spell Found

Fatal Fortune

Magical Romance with a Touch of Mystery

***

Something Magical

Curiously Enchanted

Romantic Comedy

***

Corporate Chaos Series

In Over Her Head (book 1)

Can't Stand the Heat (book 2)

Contemporary Romance

***

Reluctant Romance

Sweet Romance (Written As Annie Dobbs)

Hometown Hearts Series

***

No Getting Over You (Book 1)

A Change of Heart (Book 2)

***

Sweetrock Sweet and Spicy Cowboy Romance

Some Like It Hot

Too Close For Comfort

Regency Romance

* * *

Scandals and Spies Series:

Kissing The Enemy

Deceiving the Duke

Tempting the Rival

Charming the Spy

Pursuing the Traitor

The Unexpected Series:

An Unexpected Proposal

An Unexpected Passion

Dobbs Fancytales:

Dobbs Fancytales Boxed Set Collection

———

Western Historical Romance

***

Goldwater Creek Mail Order Brides:

Faith

American Mail Order Brides Series:

Chevonne: Bride of Oklahoma

———————————

ROMANTIC SUSPENSE

WRITING AS LEE ANNE JONES:

***

The Rockford Security Series:

ABOUT LEIGHANN DOBBS

USA Today bestselling author, Leighann Dobbs, discovered her passion for writing after a twenty year career as a software engineer. She lives in New Hampshire with her husband Bruce, their trusty Chihuahua mix Mojo and beautiful rescue cat, Kitty. When she's not reading, gardening, making jewelry or selling antiques, she likes to write cozy mystery and historical romance books.

Her book "Dead Wrong" won the "Best Mystery Romance" award at the 2014 Indie Romance Convention.

Her book "Ghostly Paws" was the 2015 Chanticleer Mystery & Mayhem First Place category winner in the Animal Mystery category.

Find out about her latest books by signing up at:

http://www.leighanndobbs.com/newsletter

Connect with Leighann on Facebook
http://facebook.com/leighanndobbsbooks

Join her VIP readers group on Facebook:
https://www.facebook.com/groups/ldobbsreaders/

ABOUT HARMONY WILLIAMS

Bio:

If Harmony Williams had a time machine, she would live in the Regency era. The only thing she loves more than writing strong, funny women in high society is immersing herself in the nuances of the past. When not writing or researching, she likes to binge-watch mystery shows and spend time with her one-hundred-pound lapdog in their rural Canadian home. For glimpses into the secrets and settings of future *Lady Katherine Regency Mystery* books, sign up for her newsletter   at http://www.harmonywilliams.com/newsletter.

Made in the USA
Monee, IL
02 November 2020

46618968R00195